William Jane, William Jenkyn

The Present Separation Self-condemned

and proved to be schism - as it is exemplified in a sermon preached upon

that subject, by Mr. W. Jenkyn, and is further attested by divers others of

his own persuasion

William Jane, William Jenkyn

The Present Separation Self-condemned
*and proved to be schism - as it is exemplified in a sermon preached upon that
subject, by Mr. W. Jenkyn, and is further attested by divers others of his own
persuasion*

ISBN/EAN: 9783337775537

Printed in Europe, USA, Canada, Australia, Japan

Cover: Foto ©Andreas Hilbeck / pixelio.de

More available books at **www.hansebooks.com**

THE
𝕻𝖗𝖊𝖘𝖊𝖓𝖙 𝕾𝖊𝖕𝖆𝖗𝖆𝖙𝖎𝖔𝖓

SELF-CONDEMNED,

And Proved to be

SCHISM:

As it is Exemplified in a *Sermon* Preached
upon that Subject, by

Mr. *W. J. E N K Y N:*

And is further attested by divers others of his
own Persuasion.

All produced in Answer to a

LETTER from a *FRIEND.*

William Jane

MANTON on JAMES, pag. 404.
*True Wisdom, as it will not sin against Faith by
Error, so not against Love by Schism.*

LONDON,
Printed for *Edward Croft* at the *Seven Stars* in
Little Lumbard Street. 1678.

S I R,

UPon the Difcourfe that paffed not long fince betwixt you and me, concerning the prefent Differences amongft us in this Nation, and the Difficulties you then preffed me with, about the Nature and Reafons of *Schifm*, and the Side which the Sin of it would lie upon ; I began to confider of it, and forthwith refolved to fee what I could meet with of that Subject amongft that Party you fo boldly charge with it, efpecially before their exclufion, when they might be fuppofed to fpeak impartially. And amongft the reft, having procured of a Friend the Notes of a *Sermon* long fince preached by Mr. *Jenkin*, I diligently read it over, and thought it a Difcourfe very well calculated to bring this matter to an iffue betwixt us : for which end, having compared it with and corrected it by what he afterward printed upon that Text, I did refolve to fend it to you. This, I confefs, I the rather pitched upon, as he is yet alive, and is able to juftifie it ; and becaufe you alfo urged me with fome Objections offered in particular againft him, and his proceedings in the cafe, and did af-

B   firm,

firm, That he, with the reft of his Brethren, durft not now own what they had formerly preached, or preach what they formerly did about *Separation*, left they fhould revive what they hope is by this time forgotten, and difquiet the Afhes of the old *Nonconformifts*, whofe Followers they profefs to be, but herein, as you faid, widely differ from.

I muft confefs my felf not to have been a little difturbed at thofe Paffages that you produced out of fome of them, and could not but tranfcribe that from Mr. *Calamy*, in his *Apologie againft an unjuft Invective*, pag. 10. viz. *What will Mr. Burton fay to old Mr. Dod, Mr. Hilderfham, Mr. Ball, Mr. Rath-band, &c ? Did not thefe Reverend Minifters fee the Pattern of Gods Houfe ? And yet it is well known, that they wrote many Books againft thofe that refufed Communion with our Churches* (he means the *Epifcopal*), *and were their greateft Enemies.* And I cannot forget another you fhewed me out of the *Vindication of the Presbyterial Government*, pag. 135. publifhed by the *Provincial Affembly of London*, 1650. (of whom you told me Mr. *Jenkin* was one) viz. *There were many godly and learned Nonconformifts of this laft Age, that were perfuaded in their Confciences, that they could not hold Communion with the Church of* England *, in receiving the Sacrament kneeling, without fin ; yet did they not feparate from her.*

her. Indeed, in that particular Act they withdrew; but yet so, as that they held Communion with her in the rest; being far from a negative, much more from a positive Separation. Nay, some of them, even when our Churches were full of sinful Mixtures, with great Zeal and Learning defended them so far, as to write against those that did separate from them.

I do acknowledge, that I am not able to reconcile all things of this nature, and that it is very hard to shew where the difference lies betwixt now and then, and to find out what the People have to scare them from Communion with the *Church of England* now, that they had not in those Times; and why what Mr. *Cartwright*, Mr. *Dod*, &c. wrote then in defence of it, will not still so far hold good. But I hope you easily conceive, that the Case is not the same with the *Ministers* as the *People*. For the *People*, it is confessed, and you gave me an undeniable Proof of the general Belief of the present *Nonconformists* in this matter, *viz.* That when by the late *Act of Parliament* every one that was in any Office of Trust was required to receive the *Sacrament* of the *Lords Supper* according to the usage of the *Church of England*, they that amongst them were concerned, were generally advised to it by their own *Pastors*, and few, if any, were found to refuse it; which doubtless they would have done, if

either

either *they* or their *Paſtors* had thought that they had ſinned in ſo doing ; and their own Intereſt, or the capacity they might be in of doing better. Service in their Places, than out of them, would not have made it lawful, if it had not been thought lawful in it ſelf.

And therefore I do very readily grant this. But withal I hope you do perceive, that there is a great difference betwixt the *People* and their *Miniſters*, betwixt the Peoples Communicating with, and the Miniſters Officiating in the *Church* : for the *Miniſters* are in order to this required to renounce the *Covenant*, and to *aſſent and conſent* to the uſe of the *Liturgie.* And therefore, though the People may now Communicate upon the ſame terms that the People did before the Wars (when *Separation* from the *Church of England* was proved to be *Schiſm* by the great *Nonconformiſts* of thoſe Times, as is aboveſaid), and the *Miniſters* may now Communicate upon the ſame terms as the *People*, yet they cannot do it as *Miniſters* ; and what reaſon is there that they ſhould degrade themſelves, who are (as Mr. *Jenkin* ſaith, on *Jude, pag.* 21.) *Church-Officers betruſted with the ordering of the Church, and for opening the Doors of the Churches Communion, by the Keys of Doɛɬrine and Diſcipline* ; and be no more than private Chriſtians, that have no power

i.1

in thefe matters, as he there obferves ? Is this nothing, to be, from *Rulers* of the Flock, turned down
amongft the *common Herd*; and from being keep-
ers of the Keys, to be brought under the power
of them ?

But fuppofing that they could thus far conde-
fcend, yet do you make nothing of the *Apoftles neceffity*, and *woe is me ?* or think you it fit, after fo
facred a *Character* as that of *Ordination*, that they
can clear themfelves if they neglect it ? Confider
what is written in a Book called *Sacrilegious Defertion of the Holy Miniftry rebuked*, pag. 30. viz. *If
a Vow and Dedication to preach the Gofpel, no reafon
to preach it elfewhere, when it's forbidden in your
Affemblies ? Is the alienation of Confecrated Perfons
no Sacrilege ?* You told me indeed, That fuppofing
they were under the like neceffity (which you faid
they were not), yet, that as St. *Paul's neceffity* did
not, fo neither did theirs confine them to any particular Place, Time, or Number; that Preaching
was not more fo, when it was to many, than to
few, in publick than in private, in *London* than the
Countrey; and that as the Law did permit them to
preach to *Five* befides their own *Family*, fo it did
not forbid them private Conference elfewhere; a
way that the *Nonconformifts* do fo much recommend, that one of them, in his Advice to the reft,

faith of it, *That Publick hearing without Perfonal conference, feldom bringeth men to underftand well what you fay, (Sacrileg.Difert. pag.93.)* And therefore that you couceived not how St. *Paul's Wo,* or their *Ordination,* did oblige them to flock up to the Capital City, or to betake themfelves to the chiefeft Towns, and to draw great numbers together; no more than it did before *Bartholomew* in 62, to follow the fame courfe.

But, *Sir,* I will onely ask you, whether you think it not better to preach to many, than to few; and in publick, than in corners; and in Towns, than Villages; and in *London,* than the country? In Villages People will jog on in their old way, they have neither much curiofity nor leifure; or whatever is there taught or learned, fpreads no further: But you know, teach *London,* and you teach the whole Nation; thence the Light before the Wars fhone forth into all parts; and after when *Herefies were hatched and nourifhed up under her wings, from her they fpread all the Kingdom over,* as is obferved by the *Provincial Affembly of London,* in their *Vindication, pag,* 119. and the fame way doubtlefs is ftill to be obferved, if any good is to be done. And it is the fame as to the Places of eminency in the Country. And therefore whatever becomes of the remote Parts, and the little Places,

Places, great care is here to be taken, *that the Souls in Cities and Corporations be not deferted*, as the Author of *Sacrilegious Defertion* doth hint, *p.*69. and better leave thofe to fhift for themfelves, than to leave thefe unfupplied. Which gives a very good account, why they flock fo much from the Country to the *Town*. And if you ftill perfift to demand, why it was not thought fo before 62 ? the Anfwer is ready ; for then *London* was their own, and the Pulpits were fafe, when kept by thofe that were of their own Perfuafion : But the cafe being now otherwife, if they fhould retire, and not keep up a diftinct Party, the *City* would be another thing, and the whole Nation be in danger of Infection. And then what would become of them and their Families? For there are not very many of them that were bred up to the under-ftanding of Trade, or keeping Books of Account, and that can fhift for themfelves as other Men ; and if put by that way of Livelihood, where muft they feek for it? As *there cannot be a walking, with-out a moving* (as Mr. *Jenkin* judicioufly obferves on *Jude, pag.* 447.) ; fo there cannot be an eating without Food : and how Food is to be had on their part, without Preaching, is not eafie to ima-gine.

Do you think, if they had betaken themfelves

to inftruct their Flocks, that they left, by private Conference (as the Author of the *Addrefs to the Nonconformifts* propounds, *pag.* 199.), *that thofe who now fupport them in point of Livelihood in the way they are in, would do the fame in the other way*, as that *Author* conjectures ? Nay, if they were left to the mercy of the *Act of Parliament*, which allows *Five* befide their own Family, and did govern themfelves by it, can you think that would turn to any account ?

Alas, *Sir*, you know Charity is grown cold in thefe times ; and if they put all upon that iffue, we may fay, *God* help them, for it may be feared the People will not. We know, *Sir*, and you cannot be ignorant of it, that it's a Publick way, and the being followed and admired by Multitudes, when the Members have the reputation of being joyned to a numerous and wealthy Congregation, and where Trade may be promoted, that opens the Purfes, and, fhall I fay, engages the Hearts of not a few ; and therefore if you will not allow them to preach in this way, you muft not allow them to live and eat as other Folk.

Methinks your own experience fhould open your eyes, and let you fee what difference is made betwixt him that labours in the Word, and him that doth not ; betwixt him that preacheth at fuch convenient

venient Seafons, that he may refort to the Publick
Worſhip, and is willing to ſhew, that he and the
Church of England in effect are one ; and him that
preacheth in oppoſition to it, at the ſame time with
the Publick, and thereby proclaimeth, that he and
the Church are two. Alas, *Sir*, the City-Moufe
did not more excel the Country, than one here
doth the other, in the Proviſions of his Table, and
the Munificence of his Benefactors. The one lives
by Preaching, and lives plentifully ; the other lives
by his Learning, in the ſenſe of the Scholar that
fold his Books to maintain himſelf with, as ſome
of them whom I know you love and reverence are
reported to do; and others forced to be beholden
to *Conformiſts*, that have made private Collections
for them. Theſe are they that the Author of *Sacrilegious Deſertion*, *pag*. 111. is to be underſtood of,
when he ſaith, *That the French Impreſſion of the
Councils is too dear for the Purſe of a Nonconform-
able Miniſter*. And beſides, *Sir*, is it nothing, think
you, for a Man to walk diſconſolately through the
Streets, hardly taken notice of, and his Worth and
Learning covered by his Cloak and Modeſty ; and
another in the mean time failing along, perhaps with
two or three Attendants, and ever and anon one
or other ſtepping forth to ſalute him with a low-
ly Reverence ? And is not this another material

difference

difference betwixt him that preacheth, and him that preacheth not ; betwixt him that preacheth in the one way, and him that preacheth in the other before spoken of? Nay, is it not come to this, that those they call *moderate yielding* men are scarcely endured, but even their Reputations are clancularly struck at by their Brethren ; insomuch that they are fain to carry it with more wariness, and comply more than otherwise they would, that they may not be the Marks of their Reproches? Hence, I believe, it was, that after the Book entituled *The Cure of Church-Divisions* had exasperated the Party, *Anno* 1670. the *Author*, to lick himself a little whole in their esteem, made some amends for his transgression, in his thundring Book of *Sacrilegious Desertion*, in the Year 1672. And I guess, that it is for the same reason, that when he publickly professed, *That the notorious necessity of the People, who were more than the Parish-Church could hold, moved him to preach at the same hours with the Publick; and that he met not under any colour and pretence of any Religious Exercise in other manner than according to the Liturgie, and the Practice of the Church of* England ; *and were he able, that he would accordingly read himself:* yet that he never had that read ; and since his disposal of that Place, doth preach occasionally in the Meeting-places of the City,

City, at the fame hours, where there is none of that neceffity before pleaded by him, and where the *Churches* generally rather want *Auditors*, than *Auditors Churches.* And fo much are they under the awe of this, that you know, when Dr. *Manton* himfelf was asked why he ufed not the *Lords Prayer*, he replied, That he omitted it, not that he thought it unlawful, but left by the ufe of it he fhould give offence to fome of his Brethren, and his own People. So that you fee, *Sir*, to what a pafs things are brought, and that it is as neceffary for them thus to do, as it is to retain the efteem of their Party ; and as neceffary to retain that efteem, as it is to have a Livelihood where it is wanted, or to be accounted Godly and Religious. Now, *Sir*, I know not how you may like this, to fuffer difrefpect, and want, and difcouragement ; but if you do, I'le affure you that I know but few that are of your mind. For is not Refpect to be valued before Contempt; providing for a Mans Houfe, before neglecting it ; and efpecially, when this is confiftent with, and obtained in the *Service* of *God ?*

And now I am fallen upon the thing that I perceive you would bring me to, when you charge them upon Mr. *Jenkin's Principles*, who faith, that *admiration of mens perfons, and felf-conceit, felf-feeking, and pride,* are the moft general Caufes of

Schifm,

Schifm, as I fee that he doth, *pag.* 26, 27, 28. of this *Sermon.* Caufes, you faid, as evident among them, as their *Schifm* it felf, and by which, with no little art, they bolfter it up. Thus they take to them-felves the Title of the *Servants of God,* and give to the People that of *the godly* and the *gracious* ; and for their encouragement, magnifie their *Num-bers,* and which they take all occafions to reprefent. As, a *Nonconformift* can no fooner die, but it fhall be fpread through all the *Congregations,* who are told by their *Minifters* the *Lords-day* before his In-terment, that fuch a one is lately dead, and to be buried at fuch a time, from fuch a place, where he defires them to be, and to fhew their Refpects by attending his Corps to its Funeral. In order to which, his Praifes are founded from the Pulpit, and he Sainted by fome little Poet, and his *Sayings,* that have either been ordinarily ufed by him in Di-fcourfe, or frequently dropped from him in the Pulpit, are collected; and then *Sermon, Poem,* and *Sayings* vented amongft the Multitudes crowding from all Quarters of the Town, and that are as proud to carry one of them home, as the poor Zea-lots in the Church of *Rome* are to get any Rag that hath but touched the Reliques of their Saint in a folemn Proceflion. After which rehearfal, you bid me confider, how this would look if done in the *Church of England.* But,

But, *Sir*, this is a courſe that ſeems to me not at all unreaſonable, in their circumſtances ; it being very neceſſary, that they ſhould, above all things, get the Peoples eſteem, and very fit that the People ſhould teſtifie their eſteem of them ; and why not in this way of Attendance on them ? For, *Firſt*, It's a comfort to the *Church* under the loſs of their *Paſtor*, to ſee him reſpected when dead, as he was when alive. *Secondly*, By burying their *Paſtor* with honour, and putting themſelves into Mourning, and engaging others to follow him to his Burial, they do ſhew the reſpect that they had to him in a day of Perſecution and Diſtreſs, when deſpiſed by others ; and that they continued conſtant to him to the death. *Thirdly*, It's good to ſhew the World that they are not ſo deſpicable for Quality or Number, as is pretended. And are not theſe Reaſons ſufficient to juſtifie their Practice in this caſe, and to ſhew, how it would not ſo well become *you* in *your Church*, as it doth *them* in *theirs ?*

But, I perceive, this that I ſaid laſt of all ſtuck moſt in your ſtomach, as you judged it a kind of an open Challenge and Defiance to Authority ; and you thought that you had me at a great advantage, when you ſo readily brought Chapter and Page upon me from Mr. *Jenkin* on *Jude, pag.*623. viz. *That miſerable is that Commonwealth whoſe Man-*

ners

ners have brought their Laws *under their power.* For
you confidered not, that this is fpoken of Irreligious
Perfons, and Civil Affairs ; but in the Matters of
Religion, I hope, you know better, and that the
more contemptible the Laws about thofe things are
made, and the weaker the Authority is to put them
into execution, the fafer they themfelves be whom
the Laws are defigned againft. And befides,do you
think, that Men ought not to make as publick a
Profeffion of their Religion as with fecurity they
can ; and to let *the* Power underftand, how much it
would be for their Safety and Intereft to come
over to the ftrongeft Side ? And is it not far better
for *Authority* to depend upon *Religion,* than *Religion* upon *Authority?* Where have you lived all this
while, that are yet to learn in fo neceffary a Point
of Cafuiftical Divinity ?

As for Mr. *Jenkin* himfelf, when you faid, that
he made very bold with the Reputation of others,
and took as great a liberty to revile, as to commend ;
and did produce him againft himfelf, on *Jude, pag.*
184. viz. *That it is Seducers policy to afperfe the Minifters, to caufe a diflike of their Miniftry* : and again,
pag. 394. *That the great endeavour of Seducers is, to
be magnified, or rather omnified, to have all others de-
bafed and nullified :* I muft confefs that I have nothing to fay : and that what you pointed me to in
the

the fame Book, *pag.* 5 2 1. *Take away this finful cenfu-*
ring from many Profeffors, and there will nothing re-
main to fhew them Religious ; whereas a juft man is
fevere onely to himfelf, holds ftill true. It is a great
fault in them, and what, if he hath mifcarried in,
as I hope he hath repented of, fo by his filence
upon that gentle Reproof given him in *The Vindi-*
cation of the Conforming Clergie, doth feem to own.
I muft acknowledge, that my own Temper, as well
as my Religion, hath fo much endeared me to that
moft excellent Defcription of *Charity,* 1 Cor. 13.
Charity envieth not ; Charity vaunteth not it felf, is
not puffed up, doth not behave it felf unfeemly, &c.
beareth all things, believeth all things, hopeth all
things, &c. that were all other things in the *Church*
of England as agreeable to me, as the Temper of
it, it would mightily reconcile me to it. We find
no *Martins,* no *Centuries,* no *Gangrænæ's,* no *Glo-*
cefter-Coblers, no Stories or uncertain Reports, picked up, and malicioufly improved, by which the Reputations of their Adverfaries are invaded , and
expofed to the World ; notwithftanding the Provocations they have received, and the abundant
matter that hath been formerly and of late afford-
ed for fuch an Hiftory. And there is nothing hath
made me more out of love with my old Friend
Mr. *J.* than a certain pronenefs that he hath difcovered,

THE
SERMON.

JUDE, ver. 19.

Thefe be they who feparate themfelves, fenfual, ha-
ving not the Spirit.

IN the 17 *verfe Jude* produceth the Teftimony
of the *Apoftles* of *Jefus Chrift*, in confirmation
of what he had before faid: In which Teftimony
I note five Particulars.

1. To whom it is commended ; to *his beloved.*

2. How it was to be improved ; by *remembring it.*

3. From whom it proceeded ; *the Apoftles of our*
Lord Jefus.

4. Wherein it confifted ; in a Prediction, That
there fhould be *mockers, walking after their ungodly*
lufts.

5. To

5. To whom it is oppofed, *viz.* to thefe Seducers : *Thefe are they who feparate themfelves.*

In which Words the *Apoftle* fhews , That thefe
who *feparate* themfelves from the *Church*, were
Scorners; and that thefe who were *fenfual and void
of the Spirit, did follow their ungodly lufts.* Or, in
the Words *Jude* expreffeth,

  1. The *Sin* of thefe *Seducers*, in *feparating themfelves.*

  2. The *Caufe* thereof, which was,

   1. *Their being fenfual* : And,

   2. Their not having *the Spirit.*

For the firft, their *Separation* ; Two things are
here to be opened.

  1. What the *Apoftle* here intends by *feparating
themfelves.*

  2. Wherein the Sinfulnefs of it confifts.

  1. For the firft : The Original word may figni-
fie the unbounding of a thing , and the removing
of a thing from thofe Bounds and Limits wherein
it was fet and placed, *&c.* Or it imports, the part-
ing and feparating of one thing from another, by
Bounds and Limits put between them ; and the
putting of Bounds and Limits, for diftinction and
feparation, between feveral things : it being (thus)
a Refemblance taken from Fields or Countries,
which are diftinguifhed and parted from each o-
ther

ther by certain Boundaries and Land-marks fet up to that end: and thus it's commonly taken by Interpreters in this place, wherein thefe Seducers may be faid to *feparate themfelves*, divide or bound themfelves from others, either *firft*, Doctrinally; or, *fecondly*, Practically.

1. *Doctrinally*, by falfe and Heretical Doctrines, whereby they divided themfelves from the Truth and Faithful, who were guided by the Truth of Scripture, and walked according to the Rule of the Word, *&c.*

2. *Practically*; they might feparate themfelves as by Bounds and Limits,

1. By *Prophanenefs*, and living in a different way from the Saints; namely, in all loofnefs and uncleannefs.

2. By *Schifmaticalnefs*, and making of feparation from, and divifions in the Church : Becaufe they proudly defpifed the Doctrines or Perfons of the *Chriftians*, as contemptible and unworthy ; or becaufe they would not endure the holy feverity of the Churches Difcipline, they (faith *Calvin*) departed from it. They might make Rents and Divifions in the Church, by Schifmatical withdrawing themfelves from Fellowfhip and Communion with it. Their Herefies were perverfe and damnable *Opinions*, their Schifm was a perverfe *feparation* from

Church-

Church-communion : The former was in *Doctrinals,* the latter in *Practicals.* The former was oppofite to *Faith,* this latter to *Charity.* By *Faith* all the Members are united to the Head ; by *Charity,* one to another *:* And as the breaking of the former is *Herefie,* fo their breaking of the latter was *Schifm.* And this *Schifm* ftands in the diffolving the Spiritual Band of Love and Union among *Chriftians,* and appears in the withdrawing from the performance of thofe *Duties* which are both the Signs of, and Helps to *Chriftian Unity*; as *Prayer, Hearing, Receiving of Sacraments, &c.* For, becaufe the diffolving of *Chriftian Union* chiefly appears in the undue feparation from *Church-communion,* therefore this rending is rightly called *Schifm.* It is ufually faid to be twofold, *Negative,* and *Pofitive.*

1. *Negative* is when there is onely *fimplex feceffio,* when there is onely a bare feceffion, a peaceable and quiet withdrawing from Communion with a Church, without making any head againft that Church from which the departure is.

2. *Pofitive* is when Perfons fo withdrawing do fo confociate and draw themfelves into a diftinct and oppofite Body, fetting up a Church againft a Church, or, as *Divines* exprefs it, from *Auguftine, an Altar againft an Altar :* And this it is which in a peculiar manner, and by way of eminency, is
called

called by the name of *Schifm*, and becomes finful
either in refpect, *firft*, of the *groundlefnefs*, or, *fecondly*, the *manner* thereof.

1. The *groundlefnefs*; when there is no cafting
of Perfons out of the Church by an unjuft Cenfure of *Excommunication*, no departure by *unfuffe-
rable Perfecution*, no *Herefie* nor *Idolatry* in the
Church maintained, no neceffity (if *Communion* be
held with a Church) of communicating in its *Sins*
and *Corruptions*.

2. The *manner* of *Separation* makes it unlawful ; when 'tis made without due endeavour and
waiting for Reformation of the *Church* from which
the departure is : and fuch a rafh departure is a-
gainft *Charity*, which *fuffers* both *much and long*, all
tolerable things: It is not prefently diftafted, when
the jufteft occafion is given ; it firft ufeth all pof-
fible means of remedy. The Chyrurgeon referves
Difmembring, as the laft remedy. It looks upon a
fudden breaking off from *Communion* with a *Church*
(which is a *Difmembring*) not as *Chyrurgery*, but
Butchery ; not as *medicinal*, but *cruel*.

2. The Sinfulnefs of this *Schifmatical feparation*
appears feveral ways. I fhall not fpend time to compare it with *Herefie*, though fome have faid, that
Schifm is the greater Sin of the two. *Auguft. cont.
Donat. lib.* 2. *cap.* 6. tells the *Donatifts*, that *Schifm*
was

was a greater Sin than that of the *Traditores*, who in time of *Perfecution*, through fear, delivered up their *Bibles* to the *Perfecutors* to be burnt. (A Sin at which the *Donatifts* took fo much offence, that it was the ground of their *feparation.*) But to pafs by thefe things : By thefe three Confiderations e-fpecially the finfulnefs of *Schifm* fhews it felf.

In refpect of
{
1. *Chrift.*
2. *The Parties feparating.*
3. *Thofe from whom they feparate.*
}

1. In refpect of *Chrift*, it is,

1. An horrible Indignity offered to his Body, it *dividing Chrift* (as the *Apoftle* fpeaks, 1 *Cor.* 1.15.) and makes him to appear the Head of two Bodies. How monftrous and difhonourable is the very con-ceit hereof!

2. It's Rebellion againft his Command, his great Command of *Love*. The Grace of *Love* is by fome called *the Queen of Graces* ; and it's greater than *Faith* in refpect of its Object, not God onely, but Man ; its duration, which is eternal ; its manner of working, not in a way of receiving *Chrift* (as *Faith*) but of giving out the Soul to him : and the Command of *Love* is the greateft Command, in refpect of its *comprehenfivenefs*, it taking in all the Com-mandments, the end of them all being *Love*, and it being the fulfilling of them all.

3. It's

3. It's oppofite to one great End of *Chrift's* greateft Undertaking (his Death), which was, that all his Saints fhould be one.

4. It tends to fruftrate his *Prayer* for Unity among Saints, *John* 17. and endeavours that *Chrift* may not be heard by his Father.

5. It oppofeth his Example : *By this fhall all men* (faith he) *know that ye are my difciples, if ye love one another.* Love is the Livery and Cognifance which *Chrift* gives to every *Chriftian.* If there be no Fellowfhip among *Chriftians*, there's no following of *Chrift. Let this mind be in you, that was in Chrift Jefus*, Phil. 2. 5.

6. It's injurious to his Service and Worfhip. How can Men pray, if in wrath and divifion? How can *Chriftians* fight with Heaven and prevail, when they are in fo many divided Troops? What worthinefs can be in thofe *Communicants*, who celebrate a Feaft of Love, with Hearts full of rancour and malice ?

2. In refpect of *the Parties feparating :* For,

1. It caufeth a *decay of all Grace.* By divifions among our felves, we endeavour to divide our felves from him, in and from whom is all our fulnefs. All wickednefs follows contention. Upon the Stock of *Schifm* commonly *Herefie* is grafted. There is no *Schifm* (faith *Jerome*) but ordinarily it inventeth and produceth fome *Herefie*, that fo the Sepa-

E   ration

ration may feem the more juftifiable. The *Novatians* and *Donatifts* from *Schifm* fell to *Herefies.*
Our Times fadly comment upon this Truth, they
equally arifing to both. The farther Lines are di-
ftanced one from another, the greater is their diftance from the Center : And the more divided
Chriftians are among themfelves, the more they divide themfelves from *Chrift.* Branches divided from
the Tree, receive no Sap from the Root. The Soul
gives Life to Members which are joyned together,
not pluck'd afunder.

2. *Schifm* is the greateft difgrace to the *Schifmaticks.* A *Schifmatick* is a Name much difowned,
becaufe very difhonourable : All Pofterity loads the
name of *finful Separatifts* with difgrace and abhor-
rency. He fpoke truly, who faid, *The fin and mifery
of Schifm cannot be blotted out with the blood of
Martyrdom.* He cannot honourably give his Life for
Chrift, who makes divifions in his *Church,* for which
Chrift gave his Life.

3. In refpect of *the Church from whom this feparation is made.* For,

1. It's injurious to the Honour of the *Church,*
whofe greateft glory is *Union.* How can a Body be
rent and torn, without the impairing of its Beau-
ty ? Befides, how difgraceful an imputation is caft
upon any *Church,* when we profefs it unworthy for
any

any to abide in it ; that *Christ* will not, and therefore that we cannot have Communion with it ?

2. It's injurious to the *peace and quietness* of the
Church. *Schismaticks* more oppose the Peace of the
Church, than do *Heathens*. If the natural Body be
divided and torn, pain and smart must needs follow. The tearing and rending of the Myftical Body goes to the Heart of all fenfible Members. They
often caufe the Feverifh Diftempers of *Hatred,*
Wrath, Seditions, Envyings, Murders. Schifm in the
Church, puts the Members out of joynt ; and dif-
joynted Bones are painful : *All my bones* (faith *Da-*
vid) are out of joynt. Church-divifions caufe *fad*
thoughts of heart. True Members are fenfible of
thefe *Schifms,* though artificial ones feel nothing.
None rejoyce but our Enemies. Oh impiety, to
make *Satan* mufick, and to make mourning for the
Saints !

3. It's oppofite to the *Edification* of the *Church.*
Divifion of Tongues hindred the building of *Ba-*
bel ; and doubtlefs divifion in Hearts, Tongues,
Hands, Heads, muft needs hinder the building of
Jerufalem. While *Parties* are contending, *Churches*
and *Commonwealths* fuffer. In troublous times the
Walls and Temple of *Jerufalem* went but flowly on.
Though *Jefus Chrift* the Head, be the onely Foun-
tain of Spiritual Life ; yet the ufual way of *Chrifts*

E 2   ftrengthning

ftrengthning it, and perfecting thereof, is the fellowfhip of the Body, *that by what every joynt fup-
plies, the whole may be encreafed.* When Church-
members are put out of joynt, they are made unferviceable, and unfit to perform their feveral Offices : They who were wont to joyn in *Prayer, Sacraments, Fafting,* and were ready to all mutual
Offices of *Love,* are now fallen off from all.

4. It's oppofite to the future Eftate of the *Church*
in Glory. In Heaven the Faithful fhall be of one
mind : *We fhall all meet* (faith the *Apoftle*) *in the
unity of the faith,* Ephef. 4. 13. when we are come
to our Manly age : Wrangling is the work of our
Childhood. *Luther* and *Calvin* are of one mind in
Heaven, though their *Difciples* wrangle here on
Earth.

Obfervations.

Obf. 1. *Naturally men love to be boundlefs;* they
will not be kept within any Spiritual compafs.

Obf. 2. *Our feparation from Rome cannot be charged with Schifm.* This will evidently appear, if we
confider either the *ground,* or the *manner* of our
Separation.

1. For the *ground* and *caufe* thereof : Our *feparation* from *Rome* was not for fome flight and tolerable *Errours,* but damnable *Herefies,* and grofs *Idolatries :*

latries : The *Herefies* Fundamental, and *Idolatries.* fuch, as thofe who hold Communion with her, cannot but partake of : In refpect of both which, the *Church of Rome* was firft *apoftatized*, before ever we *feparated* : Nor was there any *feparation* from it, as it had any thing of *Chrift*, or as it was *Chriftian* ; but as it was R O M A N *and* P O P I S H, *&c.*

2. For the fecond, the *manner* of our *Separation* ; it was not uncharitable, rafh, heady, and unadvifed ; nor before all means were ufed for the Cure and Reformation of the *Romanifts*, by the difcovery of their Errours, that poffibly could be thought of : notwithftanding all which (though fome have been enforced to an acknowledgement of them) they ftill obftinately perfift in them. Our famous, godly, and learned *Reformers* would have *healed Babylon, but fhe is not healed :* Many skilful *Phyficians* have had her in hand, but (like the Woman in the *Gofpel*) *fhe grew fo much the worfe.* By Prayer, Preaching, Writing, yea by fealing their Doctrine with their Bloods, have fundry eminent Inftruments of *Chrift* endeavoured to reclaim the *Popifh* from their Errours ; but in ftead of being reclaimed, they anathematized them with the dreadfuleft *Curfes*, excommunicated, yea, murdered and deftroyed multitudes of thofe who endeavoured their Reducement, not permitting any to trade, buy or fell, to

have

have either Religious or Civil Communion with them, except they received the *Beafts mark* in their *hands and foreheads*. All which confidered, we might fafely forfake her ; nay, could not fafely do otherwife. Since, in ftead of our *healing of Babylon*, we could not be preferved from her *deftroying of us*, we did defervedly depart from her, and every one go into his own Country : and unlefs we had done fo, we could not have obeyed the clear Precept of the Word, *Apoc.* 18. *Come out of her my people, &c.* *Timothy* is commanded to *withdraw himfelf from perverfe and unfound Teachers,* 1 Tim.6.3,5. Though *Paul went into the Synagogue, difputing and perfuading the things concerning the Kingdom of God ; yet when divers were hardened, and believed not, but fpake evil of that way, he departed from them, and feparated the Difciples,* Acts 19. 9. And exprefly is *Communion* with *Idolaters* forbidden, 2 *Cor. 6.* 14,17. *What fellowfhip hath righteoufnefs with unrighteoufnefs ? what communion hath light with darknefs? what concord hath Chrift with Belial ? what agreement hath the Temple of God with Idols ? Come out from among them, and be ye feparate.* And, *Hof.* 4. 15. *Though thou Ifrael play the harlot, yet let not Judah offend ; and come ye not unto Gilgal, neither go ye up to Beth-aven.* Though in name that place was *Bethel,* the *Houfe of God* ; yet becaufe *Jeroboam's Calf* was fet up up there, it was indeed *Bethaven*, the *Houſe of Vanity*. If *Rome* be a *Bethaven*, for *Idolatry*, and *corrupting of Gods Worſhip*, our departure from it may be ſafely acknowledged and juſtified. In vain, therefore, do the *Romaniſts, Stapleton, Sanders, &c.* brand our *ſeparation* from them with the odious name of *Donatiſm*, and *Schiſm* ; it being evident out of *Auguſtine*, that the *Donatiſts* never objected any thing againſt, nor could blame any thing in the *Church* (from which they ſeparated) either for *Faith* or *Worſhip* : whereas we have unanſwerably proved the *pſeudo-Catholick Roman Church* to be notoriouſly guilty both of *Hereſie* and *Idolatry* ; and our Adverſaries themſelves grant, in whatever *Church* either of theſe depravations are found, Communion with it is to be broken off. I ſhall conclude this Diſcourſe with that Paſſage out of *Muſculus*, concerning *Schiſm. There is* (ſaith he) *a double Schiſm ; the one bad, the other good : the bad is that whereby a good Union, the good whereby a bad Union is broken aſunder.* If ours be a *Schiſm*, it is of the latter ſort.

Obſ. 3. *The voluntary and unneceſſary dividing and ſeparation from a true Church, is Schiſmatical.* When we put bounds and partitions between it and our ſelves, we ſin (ſay ſome) as did theſe Seducers here taxed by *Jude.* If the *Church* be not Heretical, or Idolatrous, or do not by Excommunication,

nication, Perfecution, &c. thruſt us out of its Communion ; If it be ſuch as *Chriſt* the *Head* hath Communion with, we the *Members* ought not by *ſepa-*
ration to rend and divide the *Body.* To ſeparate
from *Congregations,* where *the Word of Truth* and
Goſpel of Salvation are held forth in an ordinary
way, as the Proclamations of Princes are held forth
upon Pillars to which they are affixed ; where the
Light of the Truth is ſet up as upon a Candleſtick,
to guide Paſſengers to Heaven : To ſeparate from
them to whom belong the *Covenants,* and where
the *Sacraments,* the *Seals* of the *Covenant,* are for
ſubſtance rightly diſpenſed ; where *Chriſt walketh*
in the midſt of his golden candleſticks, and diſcovers
his Preſence in his *Ordinances,* whereby they are
made effectual to the Converſion and Edification of
Souls, in an ordinary way ; where the Members
are *Saints,* by a profeſſed ſubjection to *Chriſt* and
his *Goſpel,* and haply have promiſed this explicitly
and openly ; where there are ſundry who in the
judgment of Charity may be conceived to have the
work of Grace really wrought in their Hearts, by
walking in ſome meaſure anſwerable to their Profeſſion : I ſay, to ſeparate from theſe, as thoſe with
whom *Church-communion* is not to be held and maintained, is unwarrantable, and Schiſmatical. *Pre-*
tences for *Separation* (I am not ignorant) are alledged :

ledged ; frequently, and moſt plauſibly, that of *Mixt Communion*, and of admitting into *Church-fellowſhip the vile with the precious*, and thoſe who are Chaff, and therefore ought not to lodge with the Wheat.

Anſw. 1. Not to inſiſt upon what ſome have urged, *viz.* That this hath been the *ſtone at which moſt Schiſmaticks have ſtumbled*, and the Pretence which they have of old alledged, as having ever had a *Spiritum Excommunicatorium*, a Spirit rather putting them upon dividing from thoſe who, they ſay, are unholy, than putting them upon any godly endeavours of making themſelves holy ; as is evident in the Examples of the *Audæans, Novatians, Donatiſts, Anabaptiſts, Browniſts, &c.*

2. Let them conſider, Whether the want of the exact purging and reforming of theſe Abuſes, proceed not rather from ſome *unhappy Obſtructions* and political Reſtrictions (whether or no cauſed by thoſe who make this Objection, God knows) in the exerciſe of *Diſcipline* ; than from the allowance or neglect of the *Church* it ſelf. Nay,

3. Let them conſider, Whether when they ſeparate from *ſinful mixtures*, the *Church* be not at that very time purging out thoſe *ſinful mixtures* : And is that a time to make a *ſeparation* from a *Church*, by departing from it, when the Servants of

F   *Chriſt*

Chrift are making a *feparation* in that *Church*, by reforming it? But,

4. Let it be ferioufly weighed, That fome *finful mixtures* are not a fufficient caufe of *feparation* from a *Church*. Hath not God his *Church*, even where *corruption of Manners* hath crept into a *Church*, if *purity of Doctrine* be maintained? And is *feparation* from that *Church* lawful, from which *God* doth not feparate? Did the *Apoftle*, becaufe of the *finful mixtures* in the *Church of Corinth*, direct the Faithful to *feparate?* Muft not he who will forbear *Communion* with a *Church*, till it be altogether freed from *mixtures*, tarry till the day of Judgement? till when, we have no promife, that *Chriſt* will gather out of his Church *whatfoever doth offend.*

5. Let them confider, Whether *God* hath made *private Chriſtians Stewards in his Houfe*, to determine whether thofe with whom they Communicate are fit Members of the Church, or not? Or rather, Whether it be not their duty, when they difcover Tares in the Church, in ftead of feparating from it, to labour that they may be found good Corn; that fo when *God* fhall come to gather his Corn into his Garner, they may not be thrown out? *Church-Officers* are minifterially betrufted with the Ordering of the Church, and for the opening and fhutting of the doors of the

Churches

Churches Communion, by the Keys of Doctrine
and Difcipline : And herein if they fhall either be
hindred, or negligent, *private Chriftians* fhall not
be intangled in the guilt of their Sin, if they be
humbled, and ufe all lawful means for remedy,
though they do Communicate.

6. Let them fearch, Whether there be any *Scripture-warrant* to break off Communion with any
Church, when there is no defect in the *Ordinances
themfelves*, onely upon this ground, becaufe fome
are admitted to them, who, becaufe of their perfonal mifcarriages, ought to be debarred? The *Jews*
of old, though they feparated when the Worfhip
it felf was corrupted, 2 *Chron.* 11. 14, 16. yet not
becaufe wicked men were fuffered to be in outward Communion with them, *Jer.* 7. 9, 10. Nor
do the Precepts or Patterns of the *Chriftian* Churches, for cafting out of Offenders, give any liberty
to *feparation*, in cafe of failing to caft them out ;
and though the fuffering of fcandalous Perfons be
blamed, yet not the Communicating with them.
The Command *not to eat with a Brother who is a
fornicator, or covetous, &c.* 1 *Cor.* 5. 11. concerns
not Religious, but Civil Communion, by a voluntary, familiar, intimate Converfation, either in being invited, or inviting ; as is clear by thefe two
Arguments.

1. That

1. That Eating which is here forbidden with a Brother, is allowed to be with an *Heathen* : But it's the Civil Eating which is onely allowed to be with an *Heathen* : Therefore, it's the Civil Eating which is forbidden to be with a Brother.

2. The Eating here forbidden, is for the punish-ment of the *nocent*, not for a punishment to the *in-nocent*. Now though such Civil Eating was to be forborn, yet it follows not at all, much less much more, that Religious Eating is forbidden.

1. Because Civil Eating is arbitrary, and unne-cessary ; not so Religious, which is enjoyned, and a commanded Duty.

2. There is danger of being infected by the wicked in civil, familiar, and arbitrary Eatings ; not so in joyning with them in an holy and com-manded Service and Ordinance.

3. Civil Eating is done out of love to the Party inviting or invited ; but Religious is done out of love to *Jesus Christ*, were it not for whom, we would neither eat at *Sacrament* with wicked men, nor at all.

To conclude this ; *Separation* from *Churches*, from which *Christ* doth not separate, is *Schismatical*. Now it's clear in the *Scripture*, that *Christ* owneth *Chur-ches* where *Faith* is found for the substance, and their *Worship Gospel-worship*, though there be many defects

defects and *sinful mixtures* among them. And what I have said concerning the *Schismaticalness* of *separation*, because of the *sinful mixtures* of those who are wicked in *practice*, is as true concerning *separation* from them who are erroneous in *judgment*, if the Errours of those from whom the *separation* is made, be not Fundamental, and hinder Communion with *Christ* the Head. And much more clear (if clearer can be) is the *Schismaticalness* of those who separate from, and renounce all *Communion* with those *Churches* which are not of their *own manner of constitution*, and modell'd according to the Platform of their own particular *Church-order*. To refrain Fellowship and Communion with such *Churches* who profess *Christ* their *Lord*, whose *Faith* is found, whose *Worship* is *Gospel-worship*, whose *Lives* are holy, because they come not into that particular way of *Church-Order* which we have pitch'd upon, is a Schismatical rending of the *Church* of *Christ* to pieces. Of this the *Church of Rome* are most guilty, who do most plainly ἀποδιειζειν ἑωυτὸς, and circumscribe and bound the *Church* of *Christ* within the Limits and Boundaries of the *Roman Jurisdiction*, even so, as that they cast off all Churches in the World, yea and cut them off from all hope of Salvation, who subject not themselves to their way. Herein likewise those *Separatists* among our
selves

felves are heinoufly faulty, who cenfure and condemn all other *Churches*, though their *Faith, Worſhip*, and *Converſation* be never ſo Scriptural, meerly becauſe they are not gathered into *Church-order* according to their own Patterns. In Scripture, Churches are commended and dignified, according as their fundamental Faith was found, and their Lives holy; not according to the regularity of their firſt manner of gathering: And notwithſtanding the exacteſt regularity of their firſt gathering, when Churches have once apoſtatized from Faith and Manners, *Chriſt* hath withdrawn Communion from them. And this making of the firſt gathering of People into *Church-fellowſhip*, to be the Rule to direct us with whom we may hold Communion, will make us refuſe ſome *Churches* upon whom are ſeen the Scripture-characters of *true Churches*, and joyn with others onely upon an Humane teſtimony, becauſe Men onely tell us they were *orderly gathered*.

Obſ. ult. *It ſhould be our care to ſhun Separation.* To this end,

1. Labour to be progreſſive in the work of *Mortification*. The leſs carnal we are, the leſs contention and diviſion will be among us. *Are ye not carnal?* (ſaith the *Apoſtle*): and he proves it from their diviſions. *Separation* is uſually, but very abſurdly, accounted a ſign of an high-grown *Chriſtian*. We

wrangle

wrangle becaufe we are Children, and are *men in malice* becaufe *children in holineß* ; Wars among our felves proceed *from the lufts that war in our members*, James 4. 1.

2. Admire no Mans *Perfon*. The exceffive regarding of fome, makes us defpife others in refpeċt of them. When one Man feems a Gyant, another will feem a Dwarf in comparifon of him. This caufed the *Corinthian Schifm*. Take heed of Manworfhip, as well as Image-worfhip : Let not *Idolatry* be changed, but abolifh'd. Of this largely before, upon *having mens perfons in admiration.*

3. Labour for *experimental benefit* by the *Ordinances*. Men feparate to thofe *Churches* which they account better, becaufe they never found thofe where they were before (to them) good. Call not *Minifters good* (as the *young man* in the *Gofpel* did *Chrift*) complementally onely ; for if fo, you will foon call them *bad*. Find the fetting up of *Chrift* in your Hearts by the *Miniftry*, and then you will not dare to account it *Antichriftian*. If, with *Jacob*, we could fay of our *Bethels*, *God is here*, we would fet up Pillars, nay be fuch, for our conftancy in abiding in them.

4. Neither *give* nor *receive Scandals*. Give them not, to occafion others to feparate ; nor receive them, to occafion thy own feparation : Watch exactly ;

actly ; conftrue doubtful matters charitably. Look not upon Blemifhes with Multiplying-glaffes, or old Mens Spectacles : Hide them, though not imitate them : Sport not your felves with others nakednefs. Turn *feparation from*, into *lamentation for* the *Scandalous*.

5. Be not much taken with *Novelties.* New-Lights have fet this *Church* on fire : For the moft part they are taken out of the Dark-Lanthorns of old *Hereticks.* They are falfe and Fools-fires, to lead Men into the Precipice of *Separation.* Love Truth in an old drefs ; let not Antiquity be a prejudice againft, nor Novelty an inducement to the entertainment of Truth.

6. Give not way to leffer differences. A little divifion will foon rife up to greater : Small Wedges make way for bigger. Our Hearts are like to Tinder ; a little Spark will enflame them. Be jealous of your Hearts when Contentions begin, ftifle them in the Cradle. *Paul* and *Barnabas* feparated about a fmall matter, the taking of an Affociate.

7. Beware of *Pride*, the Mother of Contention and Separation. *Love not the preheminence.* Rather be fit for, than defirous of Rule. Defpife not the meaneft ; fay not, *I have no need of thee.* All *Schifms* and *Herefies* are moftly grafted upon the Stock of *Pride.* The firft rent that was ever made in *God's* Family,

Family, was by the Pride of Angels, *ver.* 14. and
that Pride was nothing elfe but the defire of *Inde-*
pendency.

8. Avoid *Self-feeking.* He who feeks his own
things and profit , will not mind the good and
peace of the *Church.* Oh take heed left thy Secular
Intereft draw thee to a new *Communion,* and thou
colour over thy departure with Religion and Confcience.

Thus have we fpoken of the firft, *viz.* What
thefe *Seducers* did, *viz. feparate themfelves.*

2. The Caufe of their *feparation,* or what they
were, in thefe words, *fenfual, not having the Spirit.*

[*This I will onely give the Breviate of (ftill keeping
to his own words) leaving it to his* Commentary
on Jude, *fince printed.*]

By the word ψυχικός the *Apoftle* feems to me to
make their *bruitifh fenfuality* and *propenfions* to be
the caufe of their *feparation :* as if he had faid, They
will not live under the *ftrict Difcipline,* whe e they
muft be curb'd and reftrain'd from following their
lufts ; no, thefe *Senfuallifts* will be alone by themfelves, in Companies, where they may have their
fill of *fenfual pleafures,* and where they may grati-
fie their *genius* to the utmoft.

The *Apoftle* feems to add this their *fenfuality,*

·G   and

and *want of the Spirit,* to their *separating themselves,* not onely to shew, that *sensuality* was the cause of their *separation,* and the *want of the Spirit* the cause of *both*; but as if he intended directly to thwart and cross them in their pretences of having an high and extrordinary measure of *spiritualness* above others, who, as these *Seducers* might pretend, were in so low a Form of *Christianity,* and had so little *spiritualness,* that they were not worthy to keep them company: whereas *Jude* tells these *Christians,* that these *Seducers* were so far from being more *spiritual* than others, that they were meer *Sensuallists,* and had nothing in them of the *Spirit* at all, *&c.*

Observations.

Obf. 1. *Commonly sensuality lies at the bottom of sinful separation, and making of Sects.* Separate themselves, sensual, *&c.*

Obf. 2. *It's possible for those who are sensual, and without the Spirit, to boast of Spiritualness.* Of these before.

Obf. 3. *Sanctity and Sensuality cannot agree together.*

Obf. 4. *They who want the Spirit, are easily brought over to Sensuality.*

To his Worthy Friend H. N.

S I R,

I Heartily thank you for putting me in mind of our late Difcourfe, and for giving me fo fair an opportunity to purfue it, by the *Sermon* that you fent me ; which I greedily read, and had no fooner run over, but I blefs'd my felf to find, that you fhould put the Caufe upon this Iffue, and to appeal to *that* for the juftification of the prefent *Separation.* I look'd again, and thought that you might be miftaken, and had fent me a Sermon againft Mr. *Jenkin*, rather than one for him. It was a Difcourfe that I do acknowledge my felf not to be altogether a Stranger to, and what I then retained fome remembrance of ; but yet wholly to undeceive my felf, I fent for the Book which you fay you compared it with, and, to my no fmall fatisfaction, found them (as to what concerns the matter of our Difpute) honeftly to agree ; and that you may as well bring the one to vouch for the credit

of

of the other, as he himself may (if there were occafion) Mr. *Brinfley*'s *Arraignment of Schifm* (from
whence he hath borrowed the fubftance of this
Sermon) in the juftification of what he hath faid
here upon that Subjeft.

And now, *Sir*, I am glad that I have brought you
thus far ; for I defire no better advantage than
what this *Sermon* will afford me, and fhall decline
the Order that we obferved in our Difcourfe, on
purpofe to comply with it.

You may remember, that I then undertook to
fhew,

1. That the *old Nonconformifts* did themfelves
   hold *Lay-Communion* with the *Church of England*, and accounted thofe that did not, guilty of *Schifm*, as by their Writings yet extant
   doth appear.

2. That the *prefent Nonconformifts*, who are *Pref-
   byterians*, did plead their Practice, and ufe
   their Arguments, againft the *Independents*, and
   others, that did in the late Times feparate
   from themfelves.

3. That *Lay-Communion* with the *Church of England*, is the fame in our Times, that it was in
   the Times of the *old Nonconformifts* ; and that
   the *Church of England* hath as much to fay
   for it felf now, as it had then.

4. That

4. That therefore the *new Separation* doth not in reality differ from the *old*, and is truly *Schifm*, if either *they*, or the *old Nonconformifts* spoke true.

Now this I look upon as a very covenient Method to bring the Cafe to a Decifion ; but becaufe I will fhew how willing I am to meet you, and how confident I am in the goodnefs of my Caufe, I fhall take that courfe which will more readily lead me to make ufe of the *Sermon*, though in the purfuing of *that*, I fhall alfo fay what will ferve for the proof of the *Propofitions* before laid down.

In the firft place, it will be neceffary to fhew what *Schifm* is. Now, that, as may be collected from Mr. *Jenkin* here, *is a perverfe or undue feparation from Church-Communion, pag.* 21, 22. or, *a voluntary and unneceffary dividing and feparation from a true Church, pag.* 31.

And upon this Definition I fhall proceed, and fhew,

1. *That the Church of England is a true Church.*

2. *That there is a Separation from it.*

3. *That this Separation is voluntary and unneceffary.*

4. *That therefore the prefent Separation is fchifmatical.*

1. *That the Church of England is a true Church.*

But

But here we are put to it, to tell what the *Church of England* is, by the Author of *Sacrilegious Desertion*, pag. 35. *We are told* (faith he) *of Schism from the Church of England, when I would give all the Money in my Purse, to make me understand what the Church of England is.* I might here, without any more ado, refer him to Mr. *Baxter* for resolution; of whom, Mr. *Hickman* faith, in his *Bonasus Vapulans*, printed the same Year, *pag.* 138. *That he has Communion with the Church of England in all Ordinances*; who cannot but certainly know what that *Church* is, or else how can he hold Communion with it ? But because there is so great a Profit like to attend it, and in compassion to him that hath there raised so much dust that he cannot see his own way, I shall for once tell him what it is by Wise Men thought to be, *viz.* That Company of Persons, in this Nation, that doth joyn together in the Ordinances of God, according to the Laws established amongst us for Ecclesiastical Matters. *It is the joyning together in the Ordinances of God, which makes a Church a True Church*, as Mr. *Brinsley* faith, in his *Arraignment of Schism*, pag. 31. And it's the joyning together in them, according to the Laws established amongst us, that makes such a Church to be the *Church of England*. I must profess, Sir, to you, That I can hardly forbear to expose that

Book

Book of *Sacrilegious Desertion*, that as much abounds
with Ill-nature, Self-conceit, Confusion, and Self-
contradiction, as any that I have met with of that
kind ; but because the *Author* hath been in many
things of good use to the *Church of God*, I shall not
treat him with that rigour such a Book deserves ;
and shall therefore proceed to shew, *That this Church
is a True Church*. He indeed, *pag.* 43. of that Book,
when it had been objected against the present *separation*, That *their Members are taken out of True
Churches*, replies, *How many Bishops have written,
that the Church of Rome is a True Church, &c. and
must no Churches therefore be gathered out of them ?*
[*Her*, it should be.] thereby disingenuously insinu-
ating, That the *Church of England* is no otherwise
a *true Church* than that of *Rome*, and may as safely
be separated from. Now how the *Church of Rome*
is said to be a *true Church*, Mr. *Brinsley* will inform
us, *pag.* 26. of his *Arraignment of Schism : There is
a twofold Trueness ; Natural, the one ; Moral, the
other : In the former sense, a Cheater, a Thief may be
said to be a true Man, and a Whore a true Woman,
and (till she be divorced) a true Wife ; yea, and the
Devil himself, though the Father of Lies, yet a true
Spirit. And in this sense we shall not need to grutch
the Church of Rome the name of a true Church ; if
not so, why do we call her a Church ? A Church she*

is,

is, in regard of the outward Profession of Christiani-ty ; but yet a false Church : true in Existence, but false in Belief, &c. not so a true Church, but that she is also a false Church, an Heretical, Apostatical, Antichristian Synagogue. But whether the Author of Sacrilegious Desertion hath the same thoughts of the Church of England, let pag. 76. shew, where he faith, As I constantly joyn in my Parish-Church in Li-turgie and Sacraments, so I hope to do while I live (if I live under as honest a Minister) at due times. And he would by all means have their Assemblies accounted onely as Chappel-Meetings, pag. 15. with respect to the Publick. Now God forbid that all this should be, and that in the mean time he should think, that the Church of England is no more a true Church than the Church of Rome, and not more to be held Communion with. But the contrary is evi-dent from him, and so his abovesaid Insinuation the more blame-worthy. But however, let him think as he pleaseth, it is very obvious, that the constant Opinion of the old Nonconformists was , That the Church of England was a true Church, and what, as such, they thought that they were oblig'd to hold Communion with. So Mr. Baxter, in his Preface to the Cure of Church-Divisions, faith of them ; The old Nonconformists, who wrote so much against Separa-tion, were neither blind, nor Temporizers. They saw the

the danger on that fide. Even Brightman *on the* Re-
velation, *that writeth againſt the* Prelacy *and Ceremonies, ſeverely reprehendeth the Separatiſts.* Read
but the Writings of Mr. J. Paget, *Mr.* J.Ball, *Mr.*Hil-
derſham, *Mr.* Bradſhaw, *Mr.* Bains, *Mr.* Rathband,
*and many ſuch others, againſt the Separatiſts of thoſe
Times, and you may read, that our Light is not greater, but leſs than theirs, &c.* So Mr. *Crofton,* in his
Reformation not Separation, (though ſeveral of them
he evidently wrongs, that were far from any diſaf-
fection to the Order and Diſcipline of the *Church,*as
R*idley, &c.*) *pag.* 43. Tindal, Hooper, Ridley, Latimer, Farrar, Whitaker, Cartwright, Bains, Sibbs,
Preſton, Rogers, Geree, J. Ball, Langly, Hind, Ni-
cols, *&c. groaning under retained Corruptions, &c.
yet lived to their laſt breath in conſtant Communion
with the Church..* And this they did, upon the ſup-
poſition of this Truth. Nay, ſo far were they per-
ſuaded of this, that they did prefer it to moſt
Churches in the World. So the Letters betwixt
the *Miniſters* of *Old* and *New-England,* publiſhed
by Mr. *Aſh* and Mr. *Rathband,* 1643. *If we deny
Communion with ſuch a Church as ours, there hath
been no Church this thouſand years with which a Chriſtian might lawfully joyn.* When the Wars began,
there were thoſe indeed that talked otherwiſe, and
then they would perſuade the People, that there

H was

was no difference betwixt *that* and *Rome* ; as Mr.
Marſhal, in his *Sermon* upon the *Union of the Two
Houſes*, Jan. 18. 1647. *All Chriſtendom, except Ma-
lignants in England, do now ſee, that the Queſtion in
England is, Whether Chriſt or Antichriſt ſhall be
Lord and King?* Then thoſe that were ſuſpended
before the *Long-Parliament* time, were *the Witneſſes that were ſlain*, and the *Prelacy* was an *Antichri-
ſtian Power* ; and the *taking away of that, and the
Ceremonies*, was *the tenth part of the City falling*, as
Mr. *Woodcock* did expound it, in his *Sermons of the
two Witneſſes*, 1643. *pag.* 83, & 86. Then they
were the *Amorites*, and there was *the cup of abomi-
nation* amongſt them, as you may find it in a Book
called *The Principal Acts of the General Aſſembly
convened at Edinburgh*, May 29. 1644. *pag.* 19.
But when the Tide began to turn, and *Presbytery*
was oppoſed, and in great danger of being run
down by *Independency*, they changed their Tune,
and began to plead for the Truth of it, and their
Propriety in it. Thus we find *Ordination according
to the Church of England* maintained by the *London-Miniſters*, in their *Vindication*, *pag.* 143. *We
do not deny, but that the way of Miniſters entring
into the Miniſtry by the Biſhops, had many defects in
it :—But we add, That notwithſtanding all the accidental corruptions, yet it is not ſubſtantially and eſſen-
tially*

tially corrupted : By Dr. *Seaman,* in his *Anſwer* to the *Diatribe* ; by Mr. *Brinſley of Schiſm, page* 31. by Mr. *Firmin,* in his *Separation examined, page* 23. Then we are told, That *Preaching* and *Prayer* were kept pure in the *Epiſcopal days,* by Mr. *Firmin, ibid. pag.* 29. And to ſhew you how reverendly they ſpoke of this *Church,* I will onely quote it from one that muſt be thought to ſpeak out of no affeꞔtion, and that is *J. Goodwin,* in his *Sion College viſited,*pag. 26. *Doubtleſs the real and true Miniſters of the Province of London, having ſuch abundant opportunity of converſe with Travellers from all Parts, cannot but be full of the truth of this Information, That there was more of the truth and power of Reli-gion in England, under the late Prelatical Govern-ment, than in all the Reformed Churches beſides.*

But you will ſay, All this may be granted, and yet nothing ſaid ; for the Caſe is altered, the *Church of England* not being now what it was then. This, I acknowledge, the Author of *Sacrilegious Deſertion, pag.* 43. doth ſuggeſt ; *The love of Peace, and the fear of frightning any further from Pariſh-Communi-on than I deſire, do oblige me to forbear ſo much as to deſcribe or name the additional Conformity, and that Sin which Nonconformiſts fear and fly from, which maketh it harder to us that deſire it, to draw many good People to Communion with Conformiſts, than it*

was

was of old. But this *additional Conformity* that the People are concerned in, I am yet to underftand; and I fear he had another Reafon to forbear the defcription of it, *viz.* becaufe he could not. However, for once fuppofe this ; yet he grants, that it's onely harder ; but that doth not make it unlawful : For then what fhall we fay to Mr. *Corbet,* that in his *Difcourfe of the Religion of England, Anno* 1667. *pag.* 33. doth declare, *That the Presbyterians generally hold the Church of England to be a true Church, though defective in its Order and Difcipline, and frequent the Worfhip of God in the Publick Affemblies ?* (I believe he fpeaks of thofe that he converfes with, for here it is generally otherwife as to the point of Practice.) What fhall we fay to Mr. *Hickman,* that in his *Bonafus Vapulans, page* 133. faith of himfelf, *I profefs, where-ever I come, I make it my bufinefs to reconcile People to the Publick Affemblies ; my Confcience would fly in my Face, if I fhould do otherwife ?* What fhall be faid to that of Mr. Baxter, in his *Cure of Church-Divifions,* pag. 263, 264, 265. where he faith, *Thoufands of well-meaning People live as if England were almost all the World, and do boldly feparate from their Neighbours here ; which they durft not do, if they foberly confidered, that almoft all the Chriftian World are worfe than they ?* And that the prefent State of this *Church* is far better

ter

ter than almoſt any in the World, he there doth
largely prove. So far as the Profeſſion of theſe Perſons doth hold (who both deſerve, and I am confident have your reverence) we are ſafe.

But ſtill ſuppoſe the worſt, I will be bold to ſay,
and I queſtion not to prove, that our *Church* is
more a *Church*, than what theirs was, when they ſo
briskly aſſaulted the *Independents*, and charged them
with no leſs than *Schiſm*, for their *ſepartion* from it.
For, if you conſider, you will find, that their *Con-
ſtitution* was not ſetled, nor the *Church* in any order, when this Controverſie began, and was carried
on amongſt them. How it was in 1642. Sir *Edward Dering*, in his Speeches then made and printed, will inform us, *pag.* 47. " The Church of *Eng-*
" *land* (not long ſince the Glory of the Reformed
" Religion) is miſerably torn and diſtracted : you
" can hardly now ſay, which is the Church of *Eng-*
" *land.* A little above, in the ſame *page*, he ſaith
thus : " *Mr. Speaker*, There is a certain new-born,
" unſeen, ignorant, dangerous, deſperate way of *In-*
" *dependency* : Are we, *Sir*, for this *Independent*
" way ? Nay, (*Sir*) are we for the elder Brother of
" it, the *Presbyterial* Form ? I have not yet heard
" any one Gentleman within theſe Walls ſtand up-
" and aſſert his Thoughts here, for either of theſe
" Ways : And yet (*Sir*) we are made the Patrons
" and

" and Protectors of thefe fo different, fo repugnant
" Innovations, &c. How it was in 1645. you may
guefs, when the Sovereign Argument they had was,
That they had hopes of a Settlement. So Mr. *Ca-*
lamy, in a *Faſt-Sermon* preached that Year, " did
" call upon his People to be afhamed and confound-
" ed, as for divers other things, fo, amongft the reft,
" for this, that whilſt the *Parliament* is fitting, and
" labouring to fettle things, and while the Aſſem-
" bly of *Miniſters* are ftudying to fettle *Religion*,
" and labouring to heal our Breaches , that any
" fhould be feparating from us : as we may learn
out of *The Door of Truth opened*, pag. 5. So again,
pag. 6. " They engage themfelves into feparated
" Congregations, and do not wait and tarry to fee
" what Reformation the *Parliament* will make. So
it is confeſſed by the *London-Miniſters*, in their *Let-*
ter to the Aſſembly, pag. 2. *Jan.* 1. 1645. " That the
" Reformation of *Religion* is not yet fetled among
" us according to the *Covenant* ; and urge it to
fhew, that the Defires and Endeavours of the *Inde-*
pendents for a *Toleration* at that time , were very
unreafonable. How it was in 1646. you may fee
in Mr. *Brinſley's Arraignment*, pag. 48, 49. " It is
" alledged, That in this Kingdom at prefent there
" is no way laid forth for the Churches to walk in :
" And then, why may they not take liberty to fet
" up

" up their way, as well as others theirs ? *Anfw.* Sup-
" pole the Church hath not her way laid out, yet
" it will not be denied, but that fhe hath been all
" this while feeking it out, *&c.* Neither can it be
" truly faid, that the Church is fo wholly deftitute
" of a way to walk in, whether for Worfhip, or
" Government; the former of which is (and for
" fome good time hath been) fully agreed upon :
" the latter, however not fully compleated, yet is
" it for fubftance both determined and held forth.
How it was 1656. Dr. *Drake*, in his *Bar to Free
admiffion*, doth acknowledge, *pag.* 132. " How ma-
" ny Congregations have for ten or twelve Years
" together affembled conftantly at the Word and
" Prayer, without the Lords Supper, yea fome of
" them haply without Baptifm : A great fault, I
" grant; but, I hope, not fo great as to unchurch
" them. To favour whom, he is drove to affirm,
That " I dare not fay, the Sacraments are effential
" Notes of the Church vifible. This was that which
lay hard upon them, and what the *Independents*
took great advantage of, *viz.* That they were fome
Years without any fetled Conftitution, and at laft
fo defective in fuch a confiderable part as Government and Difcipline. So it was urged by the Five
Diffenting Brethren, in their *Apologetical Narration*, 1643. *pag,* 23. When the others charged them
with

with *Schifm*, they thus anfwer : " *Schifm*, which
" yet muft either relate to a differing from the
" former Ecclefiaftical Government of this Church
" eftablifhed; and then, who is not involved in it,
" as well as we ? or, to the Conftitution and Go-
" vernment that is yet to come ; and until that be
" agreed on, eftablifhed, and declared, and actu-
" ally exift, there can be no guilt or imputation of
" *Schifm* from it. This was what the *Presbyterians*
themfelves lamented ; as the *Norwich-Minifters,* in
their *Hue and Cry after Vox Populi,* Anno 1646.
pag. 31. " We could wifh fome Penal Law were
" againft the *Independents, Anabaptifts,* and fome
" Government fetled. And when it is objected
there, " The Parliament hath given full Power and
" Authority for Ordination,&c. They anfwer, " For
" what, Sir ? to Ordain Paftors for each Congre-
" gation ? or to chufe Elders ? In what Ordinance
" is this Power given to any but the City of Lon-
" don ? The want of this, was what their Adverfaries did continually object ; and this was what
they ufed all their skill to refute, as Mr. *Brinfley,*
pag. 31. Object. *We want an Ordinance,* viz. *Difcipline.* So in *Knutton's Seven Queftions about Separation,* 1645. And which Mr. *Firmin* is fo pefter-
ed with, that he anfwers it after this fort, in his *Separation examined, pag.* 28, 29. " But this Objecti-
" on

" on hath no place in thefe *Churches* ; for, *Prayer,*
" *Preaching, Adminiftration of the Sacraments,* yea,
" *Difcipline* they had in the *Epifcopal* days, *&c.* As
if that were fufficient to vindicate what they wanted in theirs.

The Cafe then was plainly thus : That they were
fome Years without any *fetled Conftitution* ; That
though the *Province of London* was by an *Ordinance,*
1645. divided into Twelve *Claffical Elderfhips,* yet
after all the *Ordinances* about it, the very *Form* of
Government was not ordered to be publifhed till
29 *Aug.* 1648. nay, nor the *Articles* of *Religion*
agreed to be printed till about a Month before :
And yet notwithftanding, then the Cry was, *Inde-*
pendency a great Schifm, and *worfe than Popery,* (as
Adam Steuart in his *Zerubbabel to Sanballat, p.* 53.)
and *Separation* from them, *Schifmatical.* Now, if it
muft be fo, when no body knew what the *Church*
was, nor they themfelves knew what Foundation
to lay it upon (if *J. Goodwin,* in his *Sion College vi-*
fited, pag. 10. or *J. L.* in his *Plain Truth,* pag. 6.
are to be believed, and as Mr. *Brinfley, pag.*49. dcth
not deny) ; then what muft it not be, when it is
from a *Church* that is eftablifhed, and whofe Articles, Conftitutions, and Orders are, and have been
time out of mind fetled, as ours is ? If in 1647.
there was a *Church,* and a *Church of England,* as the

I   *Minifters*

Ministers sent by the *Parliament* in that Year to *Oxford* did maintain, and as the *Form of Church-Government to be used in the Church of England,* printed by Order of *Parliament,* 1648. doth acknowledge; then certainly such a thing there is now to be found.

To conclude this: If the *old Nonconformists* thought the *Church of England* to be a true *Church*, and what they did think themselves obliged to hold Communion with; If the present *Nonconformists,* when time was, did declare as much; If the *Church of England* doth not now differ from what it was when they so thought of it; and that it is much more a *Church,* than what that was that the *Independents* were accounted by them *Schismaticks* for withdrawing from: Then I hope their *Separation* from us, will be allowed to be *unwarrantable.*

And now I know not what can be said, unless, with the Author of *Sacrilegious Desertion,* pag. 33. it be said, that this is onely *local distinction, not separation.* But that is the second thing I shall proceed to shew.

2. *There is a Separation from the Church of England.* If there was no more to be said in this Case, than what *Adam Steuart,* in his *Zerubbabel to San-ballat,* wrote against the *Independents,* 1644. it would be sufficient; *viz.* " If ye be not separated
" from

" from us, but entertain Union and Communion
" with us, what need ye more a *Toleration*, rather
" than the reft of the Members of our *Church* ?
The pains the *Nonconformifts* took to compafs, and
the joy which they expreffed at obtaining a *Tolera-*
tion, fhews that they were not of its Communion.
But what credit can we give to fuch a Declaration ? " For alas, (as Mr. *Brinfley*, *pag.* 28. faith in the
" fame cafe) what meaneth the lowing of the Oxen,
" and the bleating of the Sheep ? I mean, the con-
" fufed noife of our leffer and greater Divifions ?
" —Divifions, not onely without Separations, Sects,
" and Factions ; but Divifions of an higher na-
" ture, amounting to no lefs than direct Separati-
" on; and that not barely to a negative, but to a
" pofitive Separation, to the fetting up of Altars
" againft Altars, Churches againft Churches. That
" it is fo *de facto*, I think it will not, it cannot be
" denied.   For, if Mr. *Baxter*, and fome others,
fhall profefs, That they meet not at the fame hour
with the Publick, *under any colour and pretence, in*
any Religious Exercife, than according to the Liturgie ;
and yet in the mean time ufe it not: *the Dividers*
will not fee (as the Author of *Sacrilegious Defertion*
faith, *pag*, 20.) *the different Principles on which they*
go, while their Practice feemeth to be the fame. But
if we fhould grant this, to thofe that are willing to

I 2

hold

hold Communion with us; yet thefe are very few, to what do wholly decline and deny it. Mr. *Jen-kin* here faith, *pag.* 22. That *Separation* appears " in the withdrawing from the performance of thofe " Duties which are both the Signs of, and Helps to " *Chriftian Unity*, as *Prayer, Hearing, Receiving of* " *Sacraments, &c.* And that " *Schifm* is negative, " when there is onely a fimple feceffion, *&c.* with- " out making head againft that *Church* from which " the departure is; or pofitive, when Perfons fo " withdrawing do fo confociate and draw them- " felves into a diftinct and oppofite Body,fetting up " a Church againft a Church. Now I dare appeal to all that know them, whether Mr. *Jenkin*, and the far greater part of his Brethren, have been ever feen in our *Congregations* (unlefs at fome times the more adventurous of them have thruft their Heads in at the Door; when, if they heard all, as it is ufually but very little of the *Sermon* that they have patience to hear, Mr. *Brinfley* will tell them, That *as for Occafional hearing, it is agreed on all hands, it is not properly an act of Church-Communion,*pag.35.) And I will appeal to your Eyes, whether they do not conftantly keep up their *Meetings* in oppofition to thofe of the *Church*. But what need I go fo far about, when this is not onely acknowledged, but defended? See Mr. *Wadfworth*, in his *Separation yet*

no

no Schifm, Epiſt. to the Reader, where he puts the Caſe of the *Nonconformiſts* thus : " There are ſome " hundreds of true Miniſters of *Jeſus Chriſt,*—and " there are many thouſands likewiſe of viſible Pro- " feſſors of *Chriſtianity,* do willingly hear and joyn " with theſe *Miniſters* in the *Worſhip* of *God,* and " in a *participation* of *Sacraments :*—Theſe meet in " *diſtin̄ct Congregations,* ſeparate from the *legally-* " *eſtabliſhed Congregations* in the Land, with whom " they will not, becauſe they cannot hold Commu- " nion. And now it is out, and what you ſee is plainly avowed : So that I have leave to paſs to the next Head.

3. *That this Separation is voluntary, and unneceſ-* *ſary.* The ſin of *Schifm,* will all ſay, is very great, and *what cannot be blotted out with the blood of Martyrdom,* as Mr. *Jenkin* here ſaith, *pag.* 26. one ſpoke very well. But, as he obſerves from *Muſculus,* pag. 31. *There is a double Schifm, the one bad, the other good ; the bad is that whereby a good Union, the good whereby a bad Union is broken aſunder.* And of what ſort the *preſent Separation* is, comes now to be tried , which I ſhall do, by making my Obſervations from what this *Sermon* will afford, and by ſhewing from thence, when a *Separation* is *juſtifiable,* and when *not.* From all which, if it ap-pears , that the Reaſons produced by them fall within

within the compaſs of the Negative, but hold not as to the Affirmative, it will appear, That *their Separation is voluntary, and unneceſſary.* Now there are Six Caſes, as may be collected from this *Sermon*, in which *Separation* is *unwarrantable*, and *ſchiſmatical.*

1. It is not to be allowed, when it is by reaſon of *Mixt-Communion*, *and admitting into Church-fellowſhip the vile with the precious.* This he handles at large, from *pag.* 33. to *pag.* 37. and ſaith, That it hath *no Scripture-warrant.* And this hath been their conſtant Opinion. So Mr. *Firmin*, in his *Separation examined, pag.* 40. " Corrupt Members there " were enough in the *Jewiſh Church*, and ſo in the " *Chriſtian Churches* ſoon after, and in the *Apoſtles* " times ; but you have no example of *ſeparating* " from them. So the *Provincial Aſſembly of London*, in their *Vindication of the Presbyterial Government, pag.* 134. " Suppoſe there were ſome *ſinful* " *mixtures* at our *Sacraments*, yet we conceive this " is not a ſufficient ground of a *negative*, much leſs " of a *poſitive ſeparation.*——This they give the Reaſon of, Becauſe " in what *Church* ſoever there " is *purity of Doctrine*, there *God* hath his *Church*, " though overwhelmed with *ſcandals.* And there-" fore whoſoever ſeparates from ſuch an *Aſſembly*, " ſeparates from that place where *God* hath his " *Church*,

" *Church*,which is *rash and unwarrantable.* Mr.*Vines*,
in his *Treatise of the Sacrament,* hath a whole Chapter, *viz. cap.* 20. to shew the unlawfulness of it, and
faith, *pag,* 235. " That to excommunicate our selves
" from *Gods Ordinances* (if Men of wicked Life be
" not excommunicate) for fear of pollution by
" them, is *Donatistical.*. So Dr. *Manton,* on *Jude,*
pag. 496. " The Scandals of Professors are ground
" of *mourning,* but not of *separation.* And Mr.*Baxter* doth speak fully to it, in his *Cure of Church-Divisions, pag* 81. " If you mark all the Texts of the
" *Gospel,* you shall find, that all the *separation* which
" is commanded in such cases (besides the *separation*
" from *Infidels* and the *Idolatrous World*) is but one
" of these two forts : 1. That either the *Church*
" cast out impenitent Sinners by the Power of the
" Keys ; or, 2. That private Men avoid all private
" familiarity with them. But that the private Mem-
" bers should separate from the *Church,* because such
" Persons are not cast out of it, shew me one Text
" to Prove it if you can. The consideration of this,
made the Author of the Book called *Nonconformists
no Schismaticks,* to quit this Argument, concluding,
pag. 16. with good reason, " That if one Mans sin
" defileth another that Communicates with him,
" who can assure himself of any Scriptural Com-
" munion on this Side Heaven? All which I have
produced

produced (and could indeed tire you with Quotations of this kind) on purpose to let you see how much the Author of *Separation yet no Schifm*, doth run counter to his own Party, and withal, how little acquaintance with this Argument will serve to shew the weakneſs and inconſiſtency of that Tract. He puts the caſe thus, *pag.* 56. " If Miniſters, or " many of the Members are much corrupted, or the " Members onely commonly ſo, but connived at, it " is a ſufficient ground for the ſound to withdraw. And for this he gives two Reaſons : " 1. Left under " the pretence of Peace, they ſhould be guilty of " the greateſt Uncharitableneſs, and that is the hard- " ning and encouraging them in their abominable " Impieties. 2. Becauſe the ſound ought, by the Law " of God and Nature, to provide for their own " ſafety,—— for they cannot but be in apparent " danger by Communicating with ſuch. Now granting the Caſe ſo to be, yet *ſeparation* will not be granted lawful by themſelves, upon the Reaſons which he there gives. I ſhall refer him for an Anſwer to the firſt of the *Letters* that paſſed betwixt the *Miniſters* of *Old* and *New England*, publiſhed by Mr. *Aſh* and Mr. *Rathband*, 1643. (as thought by them at that time very ſeaſonable). When thoſe of *New England* had ſaid, *That by joyning with an inſufficient and unworthy Miniſtry, they did counte-*

nance

nance them in their **Place** *and* **Office**, *pag.* 8. it is an-
fwered, *pag.* 11. *The* Scripture *teacheth evidently, not
onely that the People by joyning do not countenance
them in their Place and Office* ; *but that they muſt
and ought to joyn with them in the Worſhip of God* :
*and in ſeparating from the Ordinance, they ſhall ſin
againſt God.* From whence you may obſerve, That
the countenancing of ſuch *whom the Word of Truth
doth condemn, as not approved Miniſters of God,* (as
it's there ſaid) is no reaſon to diſcharge us of our
Duty ; and if *Separation* be not otherwiſe our Duty, the fear of hardning others, by our Communion with them, will never make it to be ſo. Surely
this might have been very well thought to be the
effect of the ſame Practice in the Church of *Corinth,*
where there was (as the *Provincial Aſſembly of London* obſerveth, in their *Vindication,* pag. 134.) *ſuch
a profane mixture at their Sacrament, as we believe
few* (*if any*) *of our Congregations can be charged
withal* : And yet the *Apoſtle* doth not perſuade the
godly Party to ſeparate, much leſſ to gather a Church
out of a Church : Which yet had been very neceſſary, if this Author's Reaſon had been of any force.
And his ſecond Reaſon, *viz.* Care of our own
ſafety, will alſo have no place here, if Mr. *Jenkin's*
Authority will ſignifie any thing with him ; who
ſpeaking in this *Sermon, p.* 36. of that Text, 1 *Cor.*

K   5. 11.

5. 11. of *not eating with a Brother.*, *&c.* shews very well, that it is to be understood of Civil, and not Religious eating, and gives this as one Reason for it, *viz. That there is danger of being infected by the wicked in civil, familiar, and arbitrary eatings ; not so in joyning with them in an holy and commanded Service and Ordinance.* If we follow the Apostles Precept, of having no familiar and ordinary converse with Fornicators, Covetous, Idolaters, Drunkards, *&c.* we may be assured, that we shall be in no danger of Infection by their Company in Religious Offices and Duties, where there is little or no converse, opportunity, and way for it. The case, I acknowledge, is sad, when such are to be found a-mongst *Christians*, and that Discipline is not exer-cised upon them : but I ought not to leave my Place and Duty, because such do joyn with me in it ; or to separate from the *Church of God*, because such continue in its Communion : For, this is to tear the *Church* in pieces, and the Doctrine that drives to it is very pernicious. Take the Character of it from the *Provincial Assembly*, in their *Vindication*, pag. 124. *That Doctrine that crieth up Purity, to the ruine of Unity, is contrary to the Doctrine of the Go-spel.*

But truly, the case is not so bad with us, as it is represented. I know there are some that do ob-

ject,

ject, as *J. Rogers* did in 1653. *The Parish-Churches.
are not rightly constituted, for there is in them rant-
ing, revelling,*—To whom I shall reply, as Mr. *Crofton* did then to him, in his *Bethshemesh clouded,* pag.
103. *O sharp sentence! severe censure! at one word
pronounced on all Parishes indefinitely: the Position
whence it flows had need be well proved, and the Inference well backed.* For, I must needs say, that what
Mr. *Firmin,* in his *Separation examined,* p. 42. once
said of the *Presbyterial,* is true of the *Episcopal, That
there are many Ministers that have as few wicked at
that Ordinance* [of the Lords Supper], *as ever were
in the Church of Corinth.* I must confess, that I was
pleased with the ingenuous acknowledgment of the
Author of *The Cry of a Stone,* in 1642. who saith,
pag. 39. " I freely acknowledge, that there are ma-
" ny in the Parishes of *England,* which are of a ve-
" ry godly Life and Conversation, and some that
" go as far therein, as ever I saw any in my life:
" And if I should prefer any of the Separated be-
" fore them in Conversation, I should speak against
" my own Conscience: but in the Church-state and
" Order, I must prefer the other. And I question
not, but that the State of the Church is still as
good, in that respect, as it was then; and might
have been better, had those kept in it that are run
away from it, and that by their Divisions in *Reli-*

gion, make many to queſtion, whether there be any
ſuch thing in the World. Certainly, were our endeavours rightly placed and united, there is ſcarcely
any *Church* in the World whoſe Temper would pro-
miſe more ſucceſs, than that of ours : And if we
would *deal fairly* (as *J. G.* in his *Cretenſis, pag.* 5.
once ſaid) *in comparing them together, and not ſet the
Head of the one againſt the Tail of the other, but meaſure Head with Head, and Tail with Tail*; I will not
ſay of our *Church*, as he did of *Independency*, That
if that hath its Tens, Presbytery *hath its Thouſands
of the Sons of Belial in its Retinue :* but I will ſay,
That even the *ſeparated Churches*, as they now ſtand,
are not without them, as well as we : And if they
would as well look out the Extortioner, and Unjuſt, and Covetous, and Railer, (not to ſpeak of o-
thers) amongſt themſelves, as they do pick out the
Fornicator and Drunkard, that are (as they inſinu-
ate) with us, they would find their own *Churches*
not ſo good, and others not ſo bad as they imagine.

But ſuppoſing that ſuch are in the Communion
of our *Church* (as it is not to be altogether denied)
yet is not the *Church* preſently to be blamed. Hear
what Mr. *Brinſley* ſaith, in his *Arraignment of Schiſm,
pag.* 39. "Suppoſing ſuch unwarrantable Mixtures
"have been, and yet are to be found ; yet it can-
"not properly be put upon the *Churches* ſcore.
                                        "What

" What her Ordinance was touching the keeping
" back fcandalous Perfons from the *Sacrament*, they
" which have read her ancient *Rubrick* cannot be
" ignorant. And Mr. *Vines of the Sacrament, c.* 19.
p. 233. fpeaking about the Power which the *Mini-*
ſter hath of keeping off unworthy Perfons from the
Lords Supper, faith, " I as little doubt of the Inten-
" tion of the *Church of England*, in the Rule given
" to the *Miniſter* before the *Communion*, in the cafe
" of fome emergent Scandal at the prefent time.
The *Church* hath provided for the correcting of Offenders; and perhaps there may be as good reafon
why the Cenfures of it are not now executed, as
there was in the late Times. Mr. *Crofton* once told
the *Independents*, in his *Bethſhemeſh clouded, p.* 110.
" The continuance of our difordered *Difcipline*, is
" the fruit of their difordered *Separation* from us.
I would fain be refolved in what *Adam Steuart*, in
his *Zerubbabel to Sanballat, pag.* 70. puts to the *Que-*
rie : " I would willingly know (faith he) whether
" it were not better for them that aim at *Tolerati-*
" *on* and *Separation*, to ſtay in the *Church*, and to
" joyn all their endeavours with their Brethren to
" reform Abufes ; than by their *feparation*, to let the
" *Church of God* periſh in Abufes? Whether they
" do not better, that ſtay in the *Church* to reform
" it, when it may be reformed, than to quit it for
" fear

" fear to be deformed in it? If they had taken this courfe, and had given us their help, in ftead of withdrawing from it, doubtlefs the Cenfures of the *Church* would have fignified more, and the Members of it have been in a much better condition than now they are. I fhall conclude this with what is faid by a well-experienced Perfon, in his *Addreß to the Nonconformifts, pag.* 161. "If, in ftead of this " [*Separation*], each *Chriftian* of you had kept to " *Parochial Communion,* and each *outed Minifter* had " kept their Refidence among them, and Commu- " nion with them, as private Members, in the Pa- " rifh-way ; and had alfo in a *private capacity* joyn- " ed with thofe *Minifters* which have fucceeded " them, in doing all the good they could in the Pa- " rifh,— I nothing doubt, but that by fo doing, you " would have taken an unfpeakable far better " courfe to promote the Power of *Religion* in the " Nation, than by what you have done. It's they that have in great meafure weakned, if not tied our Hands, and then complain that we do not fight. If all things therefore were confidered, I believe that they would have as little reafon to condemn our *Churches* for Corruptions in this kind, as I am fure, if they will be conftant to themfelves, that they have none to feparate from us upon account of them.

2. Separation

2. *Separation* is not to be allowed for *flight and tolerable Errors, which are not Fundamental, and hinder Communion with Chrift the Head* ; as may be collected from *pag.* 28. & 37. of this *Sermon.* So alfo fay the *old Nonconformifts,* in their *Confutation of the Brownifts,* publifhed by Mr. *Rathband, pag.* 4. " We defire the *Reader* to confider, that a People " may be a *true Church,* though they know not, nor " hold not every Truth contained in the *Scriptures,* " but contrarily hold many Errors repugnant to " them. This was the Primitive Opinion and Practice, fay the *Provincial Affembly,* in their *Vindication, pag.* 139. " All fuch who profeffed *Chriftiani-* " *ty,* held Communion together, as *one Church,* not- " withftanding the difference of Judgments in leffer " things, and much corruption in Converfation. And now, that the *Church of England* doth hold no *Fundamental Errors,* I appeal to themfelves. What it was before the Wars, let the Author of *Church-Levellers,* printed for *Tho. Underhil,* 1644. fpeak : When it was objected, That the *Presbyterians,* whilft perfecuted by the *Bifhops, did hold forth a full Liberty of Confcience* ; he anfwers, This is a Slander, — *the difference between them and the Prelates being not in Doctrinals, but Ceremonials.* And therefore after the *Covenant* was taken, whilft the *Lords* had the Power of Admiffion to *Benefices,* all
Perfons

Perfons prefented were to read the *Articles* publickly, and profefs their confent to them. And that
it is the fame ftill, is confeffed. So Mr. *C.* in his
Difcourfe of the Religion of England, pag. 43. "The
"Doctrine of *Faith* and *Sacraments* by Law efta-
"blifhed, is heartily received by the *Nonconformifts.*
So *Sacrilegious Defertion, pag.* 45. " We differ not
" at all from the Doctrine of the *Church of England*
" (till the *new Doctrine* about *Infants* was brought
" into the *new Rubrick.*) And certainly, that is, if
an Error, no dangerous or fundamental one. So
Dr. *Owen,* in his *Peace-offering,* 1667. *p.* 12. "The
" *Confeffion*—of the *Church of England,* declared in
" the *Articles* of *Religion,* and herein what is purely
" *Doctrinal,* we fully embrace, and conftantly ad-
" here unto. Again, *pag.* 17. " We know full well,
" that we differ in nothing from the whole Form of
" *Religion* eftablifhed in *England,* but onely in fome
" few things in outward Worfhip. Herein too we
have the concurrence of Mr. *W.* himfelf, in his *Separation yet no Schifm, p.* 60. " If you take it [*the*
" *Church of England*] for fuch *Chriftians* onely who
" are of the Faith in *Doctrinals* with thofe that hold
" the *Thirty nine Articles* ; here the *Nonconformifts*
" come in for a fhare alfo, who are of your Faith
" therein : excepting thofe which refpect *Difcipline*
" and *Ceremonies.* And *pag.* 62. " It is evident, that
" fome

" fome fort of Errors in a *Church*, though but tole-
" rated, may be a juft ground of withdrawing;
" though I do not charge the *Church of England*
" with any fuch Errors.

This therefore being thus acknowledged, one
would have thought the Argument might be fairly
difmiffed, and that here could be no reafon found
for *Separation* : And yet when we are come thus
near, it is like the two Mountains fpoken of in
Wales, upon whofe tops you may exchange Difcourfe, and almoft come to fhaking of Hands; and
notwithftanding all, there is little lefs than a days
Journey betwixt you.　We feem to have brought
the Matter to a perfect reconciliation; but when
we leaft thought of it, we are at open War again:
For the Author laft-mentioned grants as much as
we can ask; but immediately thrufts in a Reafon
or two, that he thinks will maintain their Ground,
and vindicate their Practice notwithftanding.　The
Doctrine he hath nothing againft; but yet the *Preachers* are——Sometimes he faith, *they are contrary
one to another; fome are for the Doctrine of Predeftination, others againft it, &c. and how fhall he then
judge of their Faith and Doctrinals ? pag.* 60. Sometimes he faith, *It is conceived, many of them preach
contrary to the Articles, ibid.* Sometimes again, *It is
conceived, that feveral of them do not honeftly believe*

thofe

thofe Articles that they have profeßed to believe, p.62.
And to make all fure, becaufe it may be objected,
That the People have liberty in this cafe of complain-
ing ; he anfwers, *To what purpofe ? when fuch Er-*
rors are publickly profeffed in printed Books, and no
courfe taken for correcting or ejecting of the Authors ?
pag. 61. Things as impertinently, as flanderoufly
fuggefted. For, what though the *Minifters* differ
among themfelves in fome Points, as he doth after
his Predeceffors the *Brownifts* affirm, (as you may
fee in the *Nonconformifts* Anfwer to them, *pag.* 4.)
is that a reafon to forfake our Communion? and
doth he that forfakes ours for theirs, find the cafe
much amended? Do not the *Nonconformifts* as much
differ from each other, as any amongft us? If not,
from whence proceed all thofe Difputes about *Com-*
munion and *Non-communion* with us, about the *Im-*
putation of Chrift's Righteoufnefs, the *nature of jufti-*
fying Faith, lawfulnefs and *unlawfulnefs* of *prefcri-*
bed Forms of Prayer, of *God's Prefcience, &c.* And
why are Mr. *How,* and Mr. *Baxter, &c.* fo much
teazed by fome of their Fellows, and the latter called *Slanderer, Dictator, Self-faver,* and accufed of
Profanenefs, Blafphemy, and what not, as you may
fee in the *Antidote to his Cure,* 1670? Is it not becaufe they will not fwallow down the abfurdeft of
their Principles, or do go further toward an accom-
modation

modation of our unhappy Differences, than they will allow ?

But what are thofe Points that our Minifters thus differ among themfelves, or from our *Church* in ? Is it about the *mode* in *Imputation*, or about the *Object* of *Predeftination ? &c.* Thefe things the *Church of England* is not fo minute and pofitive in. If he will not believe me, I fhall turn him over to Mr. *Hickman* (who hath in feveral Tracts particularly concerned himfelf in this Argument, and may be fuppofed to underftand it). He, in his *Latin* Sermon *De Hærefium origine,* 1659. *pag.* 37. undertaking to anfwer *Tilenus* about the Doctrine of our *Church* concerning the *Object* of *Predeftination,* whether *maffa corrupta,* or no, faith, *Apage nugas* ; *Non folet Ecclefia Anglicana in myfteriis hujufmodi explicandis vagari in eas quæftiones, quæ nimia fubtilitate popularem captum effugiunt.* Is it about the *fpecial Grace of God* in the *converfion of a Sinner,* or the *influence* of the *Holy Spirit* in it ? Then I will dare him to produce any *that are herein Nonconformifts to the Doctrine of the Church of England,* and that teach, *That there is no fpecial Grace exerted in the converfion of a Sinner* ; or, *That the Holy Ghoft is of no further ufe in the converfion of Men, than as he firft infpired thofe that delivered the Doctrine of Chriftianity, &c.* as he flanderoufly doth fay. He may force,

L 2   and

and ferue, and wreft ; but he cannot do it honeftly and fairly. But fuppofing there were feveral
that did thus teach, and that fuch Books were Li-
cenfed where this is affirmed : Doth this prefently
make the *Church* Heretical ? Notwithftanding this,
I believe that the *Church of England* is in it felf as
Orthodox, as theirs was in 1646. when *Shlichtin-*
gius his *Comment on the Hebrews*, or what was little
better, came out thus attefted by Mr. *J. Downame:*
I have perufed this Comment ; and finding it to be
learned and judicious , plain and very profitable, I
allow it to be printed and publifhed. I doubt they
would have taken it very ill, to have been then
charged with *Socinianifm*, becaufe that Book came
out with fuch an *Imprimatur*, from him that was
deputed in thofe Times to give it : And yet I never
heard that Mr. *Downame* was correfted or ejefted
for fo doing. And may they continue Orthodox
notwithftanding,and we for fuch an efcape be count-
ed Heretical ? But how far a *Church* is concerned
in fuch Cafes, I think will appear from what is faid
in *The Divine Right of the Presbyterial Govern-*
*ment, pag.*265. " The *Church of Rome* (fetting afide
" thofe particular Perfons among them that main-
" tained damnable Errors, which were not of the
" *Church*, but a predominant Faftion in the *Church*)
" continued to be a true *Church of Chrift* until *Lu-*
" *ther's*

" *ther's* time, — as the unanimous confent of the
" Orthodox Divines confefs ; yea, as fome think,
" till the curfed Council of *Trent*,—till when, the
" Errors among them, were not the Errors of the
" *Church*, but of particular Men. Now I hope they
will be as favourable to us, and give our *Church* as
much allowance in this cafe as that of *Rome*, and
not count it the Error of the *Church*, till by fome
Decree, Canon, or Article it is owned fo to be.

Sir, You may by this time perceive, how hard
thefe Perfons are put to it, when it makes them fo
quick to efpy, and bufie to rake all the dirt they
can together, to make our *Church* deformed, and
worthy of all that defamation they have branded
it with, and of that diftance they obferve and keep
from it. How do they torture Phrafes, hale along
Expreffions, whithout due Procefs, to the Gibbet
and the Stake, and cry out *Pelagianifm*, and *Socinianifm*, nay *Mahometifm* ? Mr. *Jenkin* and his Brethren once faid, in *the Vindication of the Presbyterial
Government, pag.* 140. " To make ruptures in the
" Body of *Chrift*, and to divide Church from Church,
" and to fet up Church againft Church, and to ga-
" ther Churches out of true Churches, and becaufe
" we differ in fome things, therefore to hold Com-
" munion in nothing ; this we think hath no war-
" rant out of the *Word of God*, and will introduce
" all

"all manner of Confufion in *Churches,* — and fet
"open a wide gap to bring in *Atheifm, Popery, He-*
"*refie,* and all manner of wickednefs. And all
People would be apt to fay the fame, and could not
fee into the Reafon of this *Separation,* if it came
to this, Whether the *Righteoufnefs of Chrift* be the
meritorious or *formal Caufe* of our *Juftification?* or,
Whether *Moral Vertue* and *Grace* differ in their
nature, or onely in their *caufe?* It muft be fome-
what grofs and tangible that they can judge of;
and therefore charge them home, That they hold
no neceffity of the *Righteoufnefs of Chrift*; and, That
Moral Vertue, as it was in the *Heathens,* or in *Chri-*
ftians without any *Divine Grace,* will fave; and
you do the work : This is a *Lord have Mercy* wrote
upon their *Church-doors*; and People will be taught
by this, to avoid them as they would the Plague,
and to be as wary of trufting their Souls with them,
as their Bodies with Tygers, Bears, and Wolves.
It is truly and well obferved by Mr. *Hickman,* in
his Sermon *De Hærefium origine,* pag. 12. *Ipfa fa-*
lus non fervet eas oves, quæ æque metuunt a paftori-
bus & lupis: Once render their Paftors formidable
to them, and we may know how the day will go.
Beat up thefe Kettle-Drums, and you may eafily
gather, and fecurely Hive the Bees.

I fhall conclude this with what Mr. *Baxter* faith,

in

in his *Cure of Church-Divisions*, *pag.* 393, 394. "As
"I have known many unlearned Sots, that had no
"other Artifice to keep up the reputation of their
"Learning, than in all Companies to cry down
"such and such (who were wiser than themselves)
"for no Scholars; — So, many that are, or should
"be conscious of the dulness and ignorance of their
"fumbling aud unfurnish'd Brains, have no way to
"keep up the reputation of their Wisdom with
"their simple Followers, but to tell them, *O such*
"*an one hath dangerous Errors, and such a Book is a*
"*dangerous Book, and they hold this, and they hold*
"*that*; and so to make odious the Opinions and
"Practices of others.——And if Ignorance get pos-
"session of the ancient and gray-headed, it triumph-
"eth there, and saith, *Give me a Man, that I may*
"*dispute with him*; or rather, *Away with this He-*
"*retick, he is not fit to be disputed with.* How far
Mr. *Jenkin* is concerned in this Character, I leave
to his consideration; but if you have a mind to
inquire into it, you may repair to his *Exodus*, where
he comes like another *Samson*, shaking his Locks,
and rushing forth with his mouth full of Menaces
against the *uncircumcised Philistims*, those *audacious
Hereticks* that lie sculking in the corners of the
Church of England: but (poor man) meets with
the misfortune of that Champion, to be led away

in triumph ; and in ftead of anfwering others, is not able to defend himfelf.

3. *Separation* is not to be allowed for the *manner of Church-conftitution.* So faith Mr. *J.* here, *pag.*37. *Much more clear (if clearer can be) is the Schifmaticalneß of thofe who feparate from, and renounce all Communion with thofe Churches which are not of their own manner of Conftitution.* For which he gives three Reafons, *pag.* 38. And herein he agrees with Mr. *Brinfley,* in his *Arraignment, pag.* 32. and in his *Church-Remedy, pag.* 51. Now if this Argument held for *Presbytery* againft *Independency,* and that the *feparation* of the *latter* was for that reafon *Schifmatical,* I fee not why it fhould not be of as equal force to condemn the former, who yet do prefume to offer it on their own behalf againft us, and think that they have faid enough, when they have been able to pick fome quarrel with the *prefent Conftitution.*

4. *Separation* is not to be allowed when it is *upon thofe terms which will make us refufe fome Churches upon which are feen the Scripture-charaƈters of true Churches.* This Mr. *J.* gives as a Reafon to confirm the former, *pag.* 38. Now what thofe Charaƈters are, he tells us a little before, in the fame *page,* viz. *In Scripture, Churches are commended, according as their fundamental Faith was found, and their*

their Lives holy. Nay, he feems to refolve it wholly into the former, *pag.* 34. where he faith, *Hath not God his Church, even where corruption of Manners hath crept into a Church, if purity of Doctrine be maintained ?* Now how far our *Church* hath upon it thefe Characters, I appeal to what is abovefaid, to fhew; and for which, I queftion not but it may contend with any *Church* in the World.

5. It is not to be allowed becaufe other *Churches* are by them accounted better. So *pag.* 39. *Men feparate to thofe Churches which they account better, becaufe they never found thofe where they were before (to them) good.* Which he there condemns, and as a remedy againft it, advifes to *labour for experimental benefit by the Ordinances. The reafon of this Separation* (faith Mr. *Vines* on the *Sacrament, p.* 235.) *feems plaufible to eafie capacities, fuch as the Apoftle calls,* Rom. 16. 18. *the ἄκακοι, the fimple ; but if it be urged by the Standard of Scripture, it will be found too light.* But now the cafe is altered, and it is become a confiderable Argument ; *A more profitable Miniftry, a purer Worfhip, a ftricter Difcipline, an holier Society and Fellowfhip,* are fome of the maffie Pillars upon which the weight of this *new Separation* is laid. Hither the Author of *Separation yet no Schifm* doth with confidence betake himfelf, *pag.* 65, 66, 67. *The Reafon fuppofeth that which is*

not

not to be suppofed, i. e. *That to withdraw from a Church for the benefit of a more profitable Miniftry, is a Crime.* Now here I fhall confider, whether this Reafon will hold, and ferve to juftifie a *Separation* from a *Church* ; and, if it were granted, whether yet it is a Reafon amongft us.

Whether it is fo in it felf, let Mr. *Brinfley* fpeak, in his *Arraignment, pag.* 47. where the Cafe is put thus ; "May not People make choice of what Mi-"nifters they pleafe, putting themfelves under fuch "a Miniftry as by which they may edifie moft? "*Anfw.* Suppofe it, That a People have fuch a Pow-"er and Right to chufe their own Minifters ; yet "having once chofen them, and God by giving a "Bleffing to their Miniftry having ratified and con-"firmed that Choice, evidencing that they are the "Minifters of God to them ; whether they may "now, upon pretext of greater Edification, take a "liberty to themfelves to chufe new ones as oft as "they pleafe : this the moderate Author of the late "*Irenicon* [*i. e.* Mr. *Burroughs*] will by no means "allow, but condemns, as the direct way to bring "in all kind of diforder and confufion into the "*Church.* This both *Presbyterians* and *Independents* then are agreed in, That *Edification* alone is no fuf- ficient Reafon to forfake one *Church* for another ; and that a Perfons own Opinion of his Cafe in that
matter,

matter, will not make that lawful to him, which will be the unavoidable means of bringing in confusion to the Churches which he either leaves, or joyns himself to. But the Author of *Separation yet no Schism* thinks he hath sufficient Reason for his Opinion, who doth thus argue, *viz.* " You call it " a Crime, because you suppose it is a transgression " the Law of visible Communion with some parti- " cular *Church*: But I say, That the Laws of visible " Communion with this or that particular *Church*, " are but *positive*, and therefore subordinate to " Laws more *natural* and *necessary*; such is that " wherein we are commanded to take care of our " Souls and Salvation *:* So that if *Christians* do shift " particular *Churches*, for the obtaining of very ap- " parent advantages to their Salvation, above what " they have had where they were, I see therein no " Crime at all committed. I grant indeed, that *positive Laws* must give way to *natural*; but then there must be a plain necessity that must intervene, to make them inconsistent: for otherwise, both remain in force, as I conceive they do in the Instance here given. If indeed Salvation was inconsistent with, or what we run the apparent hazard of, in Communion with a particular *Church*, then there is sufficient reason for separation from it : but if it be onely that I conceive the increase of Knowledge,

or

or the engaging of my Affections, may be better attained by separation from, than continuance in its Communion, this is far from a *necessity*, and so no sufficient Reason to break it. As it is in a Family, If the Master takes no care to provide for his Children and Servants (who of old were esteemed the Goods of their Master) but that they must starve if they continue with him; or if what he provides, is such as will rather poyson than nourish them, or what is absolutely forbid (as *Swines flesh* under the *Law*): in such a case they may shift for themselves, and refuse to live with him, till he mends their Condition. But if what he provides is lawful, wholesom, and sufficient, though not of so good nourishment as might be wished, they are to content themselves, and to keep within the bounds of Duty and Observance. So it is here; If we were in a *Church* that either denied us what is necessary to Salvation, or that would engage us to do what will bring it into imminent hazard, we have an unquestionable Reason to forbear Communion with her: But when the means of Salvation that we enjoy are sufficient to it, and what we deliberate about is onely the Degree and Measure, [*what is better and fitter*] we cannot quit a *Church* without sin, and our departure is *unnecessary*. And that will further appear, if we consider;

1. *That*

1. *That no further Knowledge or Edification is necessary, than what we can attain to in a lawful way; and what is otherwise lawful in it self, by taking an undue course for it, is made unlawful.* As, *Hearing, Reading,* and *Christian Converse,* are very fit Means for my Improvement; but if I for it do injure my Family, and neglect my Calling, it is so far from being my *duty,* that it is my *sin.* So to edifie my self, and to acquire a greater measure of *Knowledge* and *Christian Vertues,* is a noble and most excellent End; but if I for it break off Communion with the *Church* whereof I am a Member, I make my self a Transgressor. All which, if well considered, the falacy of our Author's Argument will appear. For, suppose I reason thus: *The Laws of particular Families are but positive, and therefore subordinate to Laws more necessary; such is that wherein we are commanded to take care of our Souls: and therefore if I neglect the former for the good of the latter, I see no Crime therein committed.* Would not this appear very conceited and imaginary? And if it's false here, it is so in the Case that he offers. The grounds of his mistake herein, seem to be, 1. That he was so intent upon the *positive Laws of particular Churches,* that he had no respect to *Church-communion* in it self, which is highly necessary; by which means he did not consider, that this Principle

ple of shifting Communion for the expectation of further Improvement, is what tends so to the dissolution of a *Church*, that he that holds it is capable of continuing in no *Communion* whatsoever; and what cannot be put in practice, but confusion in, and breaking up of *Churches* will most certainly follow. This was what they of *New-England* had experience of, and therefore provided against, in their *Platform of Church-Discipline, cap.* 3. *Church-Members* (say they) *may not depart from the Church, and so one from another, as they please, nor without just and weighty cause.—Such departure tends to the dissolution of the Body.—Just Reasons for a Members removal of himself, are,* 1. *If a man cannot continue, without sin.* 2. *In case of Persecution.* But not a word of a *more profitable Ministry,* and *greater edification.* Now if this be the necessary and constant Effect of this Principle, it cannot be true.

2. Another ground of his mistake seems to be, That the notion of a *particular Church,* led him to think, that their separation into Societies distinct from *our Church,* was no more than to go from one *Parish-Church* to another (which is also the conceit of the Author of *Sacrilegious Desertion*): This he insinuates *pag.* 66. But this is apparently false, as I have shewed in part before; and which will be further evident, if you observe, that their Agreement

ment with us in Thirty fix of our *Articles*, makes them to be no more of us (whilft they differ in the others that refer to our *Conftitution*, and which they feparate from us for, as they profefs), than that of the *Independents* made them one with the *Presbyterians*; who *in all matters of Faith did freely and fully confent to the Confeffion publifhed by the Affembly, the things of Church-Government and Difcipline onely excepted*, as they fay in the *Preface* to the *Platform of Church-Difcipline in New-England.* And much to the fame purpofe is that of the *Congregational Churches* met at the *Savoy*, 1658. But yet for all this, they neither of them think themfelves one with the other ; and the *Independents*, for their *feparation*, were notwithftanding accufed of *Schifm* by the other.

2. This Courfe is *unneceffary*, and fo *unlawful*, becaufe even in the way in which a Perfon is (whilft a Member of a *true Church* in the fenfe all along fpoken of), he may attain to all due Improvement. The Author of *Prelatique Preachers none of Chrifts Teachers, pag.* 31. to encourage People rather to fit at home than hear the *Publick Minifters,* tells them, That they might otherwife help themfelves, and that they had Means fufficient without it, *as the Scriptures, mutual Edification and Conference, Prayer, and Meditation, &c. and that, though never fo few or weak,*

weak, Chrift was amongft them. And if this would be fufficient when wholly deftitute of a *Miniftry,* I am apt to think it would do as well with one, though not altogether fo well qualified as might be defired. I fhall conclude this with what the fame Author faith, *pag.* 28. *When God hath vouchfafed a fufficiency of Means, and thofe unqueftionably lawful, though not of fo rank flefh, or fo highly promifing as fome others, for the attaining of any good and defirable End, a declining and forfaking of thofe Means (whether out of a diffidence of the fufficiency of them for the End defired, or upon any other reafon whatfoever) to efpoufe others pretending to more ftrength and efficacy, hath been ftill difpleafing unto God, and of fad confequence to thofe that have been no better advifed than to make trial of them.*

But is it really thus, that there is any fuch difference betwixt the Abilities of their and our *Teachers?* and that the obtaining apparent Advantages to their *Salvation* in that refpect, above what they could have had with us, is what they feparate for? So they would have it thought, as you may fee in the *Call to Archippus,* printed 1664. *pag.* 20, 21. *There is indeed a Miniftry, and Preaching (fuch as it is); but whether fuch as is likely to anfwer the Ends of it, judge ye. Are thofe like to convert Souls, that have neither will nor skill to deal with them*

about

about their Converſion ? So again, *When there is no better help than an idle, ignorant, looſe-living Miniſtry, (under which, God knows, we ſpeak it with grief of heart, too many, not to ſay the moſt of thoſe that are of late come in, may be reckoned) or than the cold and heartleſs way that is generally in uſe, the Coal of Religion doth ever go out.* An high and daring Charge, which he will be concerned to make good, or to ſuffer under the imputation of a foul Defamer. *Have they neither will nor skill to convert Souls ?* From whence then proceed thoſe moſt excellent and laborious *Sermons* that the Wiſeſt of the Nation do ſo extol the preſent Generation for ? Whence was it, that when we were bewildred with Phraſes, and *Religion* made hard and unintelligible, and *Caſes* intricate and perplexed, that the things of it were made eaſie, and to lie near to Mens Underſtandings ; and that the part of *Caſuiſtical Divinity* is not near ſo cumberſom as it was in the days of ſome Men ? Are they *idle and ignorant ?* From whence then is it that their Adverſaries of all ſorts are ſo well oppoſed, not to ſay confuted, that they are made to quit their ground, and to betake themſelves to new Principles in their own defence ; to fall from the *Infallibility of the Perſon,* to that of *Tradition,* as they do abroad ; from old *Nonconformity,* to *Browniſm ;* and from *Preſbyterianiſm* to *In-*

N   *dependency,*

dependency, as fome do at home? In what Age and Church have the great Truths and Principles of our *Religion* been more effectually confidered, more diligently fearched into, more clearly ftated and explained, or more fuccefsfully defended, than in ours; and which I may challenge the whole Party of the *Separation* to fhew any thing equal to? From whence comes all this to pafs, if our *Church* did fo abound with *uncatechifed Upftarts, poor Shrubs, and empty and unaccomplifhed Predicants*, as Mr. *Jenkin*, with an *holy indignation*, doth in his *Exodus*, p. 55. complain? Surely if thefe Men had but duly weighed things, and had been converfant in the Writings of our *Church*, or looked amongft themfelves, they would not have dared thus to reproch the moft Learned and Induftrious *Miniftry* that perhaps *England* ever yet had. Let me recommend to fuch, what Mr. *Baxter* faith in the like cafe, in his *Explication of Paffages in the Profeffion of the Worcefterfhire Affociation*, printed 1653. pag. 110. *I defire thofe Brethren that object this, but to fearch their hearts and ways, and remember what may be faid againft themfelves, and caft the beam firft out of their own eye; at leaft to cenfure as humble men, that are fenfible of their own mifcarriages and imperfections.* And if they did according to this advice, I am perfwaded that they would think there were as good and

ufeful

useful Men in the World as themselves. Do we not find some of themselves forced to acknowledge as much? Consult *Sacrilegious Desertion, pag.* 86. *I really fear, left meer Nonconformity hath brought some into reputation as consciencious, who by weak Preaching will lose the reputation of being judicious, more than their silence lost it.* And a little after, speaking of their own *Ministers,* he saith, *Verily the injudiciousness of too many among you, is for a lamentation:* And, *pag.* 88. he adds, *Through Gods mercy, some Conformists preach better than many of you can do.* Truly when I consider what a Stock of worthy and accomplished Persons in that Quality, whether for Sobriety and Learning, our *Church* is at present furnished with, (though it must be confessed, there are that are defective in both; as when were they not?) I look upon Men of this quarrelsom temper, to be such as are described in *Sacrilegious Desertion, pag.* 91. *That having set themselves in a dividing way, secretly do rejoyce at the disparagement of Conformists, and draw as many from them as they can;* and that therefore deserve the Character he there gives, That *they are but destroyers of the Church of God:* Such that to strengthen themselves, and carry on their own Interest, care not what they do or say; but how worthily, let the Author of *the Antidote to Mr. Baxter's Cure* judge, who

N 2   faith,

faith, *pag.* 20. *That to reproch a whole Party, for the mifcarriages of fome few, without taking notice how many faults are in thofe whom they would defend, is the ufual artifice of fuch that think themfelves concerned, upon any wretched terms whatfoever, to maintain an ill Caufe, and have proftituted their Confciences to defend an Argument.* I will leave fuch to confider what Mr. *Watfon* faith, in his *Sermon of God's Anatomy upon the Heart, pag.* 167. which is fo fevere, that I care not to tranfcribe.

But to proceed: As little reafon is there to feparate from a *Church* for *remifnefs of Difcipline.* This the Author of *Separation yet no Schifm* faith that *he feeth no fin in, pag.* 67. for the Reafon given before ; and to which my abovefaid Anfwer, and what I have alfo faid *pag.* 66. will be fufficient. I fhall onely add, That care is taken by our *Church* and *Conftitution* (as I have already fhewed) for the due Adminiftration of *Difcipline:* And if it be objected, That it fails in the *exercife* and *application* of it ; I will anfwer with Mr. *Jenkin* here, *pag.* 33. *Let them confider, whether the want of purging and reforming of Abufes, proceed not rather from fome unhappy and political reftrictions—in the exercife of Difcipline, than from the allowance or neglect of the Church it felf.* If you would fee more of their Opinion formerly as to this cafe, I refer you to Mr.

Mr. *Brinſley*, in his *Arraignment of Schiſm, pag.* 32. to Mr. *Firmin*, in his *Separation examined, pag.* 28. the *Confutation of the Browniſts,* publiſhed by Mr. *Rathband, pag* 18. and Mr. *Vines on the Sacrament, pag.* 22.

6. We muſt not *ſeparate* from a *Church* as long as *Chriſt holds Communion with it.* So Mr. *Jenkin* here, *pag.* 36. ſaith; *Separation from Churches from which Chriſt doth not ſeparate, is Schiſmatical.* So Mr. *Vines on the Sacrament, pag.* 242. "If God af-
" ford his Communion with a Church by his own
" Ordinances, and his Grace and Spirit, we are not
" to ſeparate. It would be unnatural and peeviſh
" in a Child to forſake his Mother, while his Fa-
" ther owns her for his Wife. Now whether *Chriſt*
holds not Communion with our *Church,* I refer you
to the ſeveral Marks given in this *Sermon* by Mr.
Jenkin, p. 32. ſuch as *the having the Goſpel of Salvation preached in an ordinary way, &c.* which you
may compare with what is ſaid in the *Vindication
of the Provincial Aſſembly, pag,* 141. And ſo much
is expreſly granted by *T. P.* or rather *D.* (as Mr.
Crofton unriddles it) in his *Jerubbaal* (wrote in anſwer to Mr. *Crofton,* 1662.) *pag.* 18. " The Eſſen-
" tials conſtitutive of a True *Church* are, 1. The
" Head. 2. The Body. 3. The Union that is be-
" tween them: Which three concurring in the
" *Church*

" *Church of England, Chrift* being the profeffed
" Head, She being *Chrifts* profeffed Body, and the
" *Catholick Faith* being the Union-bond whereby
" they are coupled together, She cannot in juftice
" be denied a True (though, God knows, far from
" a pure) *Church.* So much is granted by the Author of *Nonconformifts no Schifmaticks, pag.* 13. who
having ftarted an Objection, *viz.* " You own the
" *Church of England* to be a true *Church of Chrift* ;
" and if fo, *Chrift* is in it, and with it ; and why
" will you leave that *Church* from which *Chrift* is
" not withdrawn ? Replies after this fort : " We
" acknowledge the *Church of England* to be a true
" *Church,* and that we are Members of the fame
" vifible *Church* with them ; but it's one thing to
" leave a *Church,* and another thing to leave her
" external Communion. To leave a *Church,* is to
" difown it, and ceafe to be a Member of it or with
" it, by ceafing to have thofe Requifites that con-
" ftitute a Member of it, as Faith and Obedience.
I will not quarrel at this time with the diftinction ;
but I do not underftand what fervice it can be of
to them, when after all the accuracy of it, fuch that
have nothing more to fay, will notwithftanding that
be *Schifmaticks,* if his own Definition of *Schifm*
hold true ; for, *pag.* 12. he faith, That *Schifm is a
caufelefs feparation of one part of the Church from*
another

another in external Communion. Now if the *Church of England* is so a *Church,* that *Christ* holds Communion with it ; and they Members of that *Church,* as he acknowledgeth: then they that leave her external Communion are guilty of *Schism :* and then it's no matter whether there be any difference betwixt leaving a *Church,* and leaving her external Communion, when the least of them makes those that are guilty of it to be *Schismaticks.*

To sum up now what hath been said : Though there be *Errors* in a *Church* (if not *fundamental*) ; though there be *corruption of Manners, mixture in Communion* ; though there be not a *perfect Constitution and Order,* and other *Churches* may be thought *better :* yet if it hath the *Scripture-Characters* of a *true Church* upon it, and *Christ holds Communion* with it, it is not to be *separated from,* and *Separation* from it is *Schismatical.* So that as far as the Negative part holds, we are secure.

2. For what Reasons may a *Church* be separated from, and Persons be justified in it ?

Dr. *Manton* on *Jude, pag.* 496. saith, *The onely lawful grounds of Separation are three, viz. Intolerable Persecution, Damnable Heresie, and gross Idolatry.* To which Mr. *Jenkin* doth here, *pag.* 23. add *unjust Excommunication,* and *a necessary Communion with a Church in its Sins.* All which I shall now consider, confider, and enquire, whether they are Caufes exiftent at the prefent amongft us, and what they of the *Separation* have reafon to plead.

1. *Damnable Herefie.* This I have before fufficiently acquitted our *Church* of, and therefore conceive that I may without more ado proceed.

2. *Grofs Idolatry.* I find thofe that deny the lawfulnefs of hearing the eftablifhed *Minifters*, are moft forward to charge this upon us. With this the confident Author of *Prelatique Preachers none of Chrifts Teachers*, that he might poffefs the unwary Reader betimes, thought fafeft to begin his Book, *viz.* "The Idolatrous madnefs of the Common-"Prayer-Book-Worfhip, hath of late been made fo "manifeft to all the Houfhold of Faith in this Na-"tion,—— As if it was a thing fo certain, plain, and notorious, that he muft not be one of the Houfhold of Faith that deth not difcern it, and abhor the *Church* for it. With the like boldnefs are we affaulted by the Author of *A Chriftian and fober Teftimony againft finful Compliance, or the unlawfulnefs of hearing the prefent Minifters of the* Church of England, *pag.* 55. printed 1664. An Author of great forwardnefs, but of intolerable ignorance or malice, that tells you, *pag.* 44. "That "our Church doth own, that Men ought to be "made Minifters onely by Lord Bifhops; (And then

then what a breach is made upon our *Church* by the *Bishop* of *Soder* in the *Isle of Man*, that takes upon him to Ordain without that Title ?) "That "the Office of Suffragans, Deans, Canons, Petty- "Canons, Prebendaries, Choristers, Organists, Com- "miffaries, Officials, &c. is not onely accounted by "us lawful, but neceffary to be had in the *Church:* And, *pag.* 45. *That Women may administer Baptism.* And, *pag.* 94. reveals a further Secret, *That the Re- formed Churches generally renounce the Ministry of the Church of England, not admitting any by vertue of it to the Charge of Souls.* Now do you not think that fuch as thefe are able Champions, and fit to enter the Lifts of *Controverfie,* that take up things by hear-fay ? By this you may guefs to what Tribe they belong; and you may learn it from Mr. *Bax- ter,* in his *Cure, pag.* 193. " It is an ordinary found, "to hear an ignorant, rafh, felf-conceited Perfon, "efpecially a *Preacher,* to cry out *Idolatry, Idolatry,* "againft his Brothers Prayers to God. But what occafion hath our *Church* given for this Out-cry ? Is it for the *Matter*, or the *Form* of its Prayers ? Not the *Matter* : for Mr. *D.* in his *Jerubbaal, pag.* 35. doth thus fay of it, *Moft of the Matter I grant to be Divine.* And Mr. *Crofton,* in his *Reformation no Separation, pag.* 25. fpeaks more univerfally ; "I "confefs their *Common-Prayer* is my Burden;— yet

O "I

"I muſt confeſs, I find in it no Matter to which
"(on a charitable Interpretation) a ſober, ſerious
" *Chriſtian* may not ſay, nay can deny his *Amen.*
Not for the *Form*: for then it muſt be either becauſe *every Form* is *Idolatrous*, or that *this Form* is
eſpecially *ſo*, or becauſe it is *preſcribed and impoſed.*
The firſt of theſe is affirmed by the angry Author
of *The Antidote to Mr. Baxter's Cure, pag.* 11. who
ſaith, " We do not think any thing to be *Idolatry*,
"becauſe it hath ſomething in it to be amended ;
" but becauſe it is uſed in the Worſhip of God,
" without any Command from God to make it law-
"ful : and this we muſt tell our *Dictator*, is a *ſpe-*
" *cies* of *Idolatry*, and forbidden in the *Second Com-*
" *mandment.* But this Author hath warily declined
the main Argument which Mr. *Baxter* inſiſted upon
three Pages before, and falls upon the Rere, and
picked up an accidental Expreſſion : for you will
find him, *pag.* 190. of his *Cure*, to reaſon after this
manner ; " Where did theſe Men learn to call their
" Brethrens Worſhip *falſe*, any more than their
" own, upon the account that God hath not com-
" manded the *manner* of it ; when he hath neither
" commanded us to uſe a *Form*, or to forbear it ?
Now I believe it would be as hard for him to find
a Command for the perpetual uſe of a Conceived
Payer, as he thinks it will be to find one for a Form ;

and

and then they that pray without a Form, are as much guilty of *Idolatry*, as thofe that ufe it : Nay, if the Divine Authority hath left it free, thefe are the *Superſtitious, that would make that a Duty commanded, and that a Sin forbidden, which is not* ; as Mr. *Baxter* there faith, *pag.* 282. But if you would fee more of this, I fhall refer you to the *Confutation of the Browniſts*, pag. 12, 13.

It is not *Idolatrous,* as *this Form* is efpecially *fo.* This indeed fome have ventured to fay, as fuppofing the *Liturgie* to be taken out of the *Mafs-Book.* So faith the Author of the *Anatomy of the Service-Book :* And therefore Mr. *Robert Baily* wrote a Book called *A Parallel of the Liturgie with the Mafs-Book,* reprinted 1661. But it fhall fuffice to fay to this, what Mr. *Ball,* in the Name of the *Nonconformiſts,* replied, in the *Letters* betwixt the *Miniſters* of *Old* and *New England, pag.* 14, 15. "The *Liturgie* was "·not taken out of the *Mafs-Book,* in fuch fenfe as "you objeƈt ; but rather the *Mafs,* and other *Idolatrous Prayers,* were added to it : for *Popery* is a "Scab or Leprofie cleaving to the *Church.*——It is "no hard Task to fhew, that our *Service-Book* was "reformed in moft things, according to the pureft "*Liturgies* which were in ufe in the *Church* long "before the *Mafs* was heard of in the World. And "if that could not be fhewed, yet forms of Speech

"generally

" generally taken (we fpeak not of this or that fpe-
" cial Word or Phrafe), is no more defiled by *Ido-*
" *latry*, than the light Air, or Place where *Idolatry*
" is committed. It is not unlawful to pray, *Lord*
" *help*, or *Lord have mercy* ; or to give Thanks, *Prai-*
" *fed be God* ; becaufe the *Papifts* fay, *Lady help*,
" or *Praifed be God and the Virgin Mary.*

Laftly, It is not *Idolatrous* as it is a *Form impo-*
fed. So much indeed is faid in the *Chriftian and fo-*
ber Teftimony, pag. 68. *To pray by an impofed Form*,
is Idolatry ; and therefore doth not fpare to fay,
pag. 70. That *Latimer, Ridley, and Hooper, and ma-*
ny other Martyrs, were Idolaters : and yet in the
mean time grants, That *they were fuch eminent Wit-*
neffes of Chrift, that they fhall come with him, and
fit upon Thrones. But I cannot underftand how *Im-*
pofition can alter the Nature of Things, and make
that unlawful which was otherwife in it felf lawful ; and I fee it is as little underftood by the better part among themfelves. So the *Nonconformifts*
Confutation of the Brownifts, pag. 15. " If Forms thus
" devifed by Men be found to be lawful and pro-
" fitable, what fin can it be for the Governors of
" the *Church* to command that fuch Forms be ufed ;
" or for us, that are perfwaded of the lawfulnefs of
" them, to ufe them, being impofed ? unlefs they
" will fay, That therefore it is unlawful to hear the
" Word,

" Word, receive the Sacraments, &c. becaufe we
" are commanded by the Magiftrates fo to do.
" Whereas indeed we ought the rather to do good
" things, that are agreeable unto the Word, when
" we know them alfo to be commanded by the
" *Chriftian* Magiftrate. So Mr. *Baxter*, in his *Cure*,
pag. 186. " If you command your Child to learn a
" Catechifm, or Form of Prayer, will you teach him
" to fay, *Father, or Mother, it had been lawful for*
" *me to ufe this Form, if neither you nor any body had*
" *bid me ; but becaufe you bid me, it is unlawful.* O,
" whither will not partiality lead men ! And it will
be worth your while, to fee how Mr. *Brinfley*, in
his *Church-Remedy*, argues againft it, where he con-
cludes, That *amongſt all the monſtrous and miſ-ſhapen*
Conceptions which theſe brooding Times have hatched
and brought forth, I do not know any more prodigious
than this, viz. That things indifferent in themſelves,
are made unlawful by being commanded. And then
much lefs are they thereby made Idolatrous. If our
Liturgie then is good for the *Matter*, and that the
Matter is not altered by the *Form* ; then you may
fee where the Storm will fall, and what they are
to be thought of that are guilty of thefe Reproches,
and how much they diftruft the goodnefs of their
Caufe, that betake themfelves to fuch Arts as thefe
to fupport it.

3. A

3. A *Church* may be feparated from upon *intolerable Perfecution.* Where I fhould confider, whether it be *Perfecution*, before I proceed to enquire whether it be *intolerable.* But becaufe I have no mind to aggravate the Cafe, by fhewing what hath been by them formerly thought *Perfecution*, and what not, I fhall omit that part of it, and enter upon the other, *viz.* the *intolerablenefs* of what is fuffered, as a Reafon for which they fuppofe themfelves compelled to quit Communion. And it muft arife to *this degree*, or elfe it will not juftifie a *Separation : Perfecution* alone will not warrant it, unlefs it comes to be *infufferable.* Now this muft be cither on the part of the *Minifters*, or on the *People.* Not on the *Minifters :* for all the difference betwixt them and the People is, that they are required to lay down the prefent Exercife of their *Miniftry*, till they are fatisfied in the fubmiffion they muft give to the Rules and Orders of the *Church* : But this is no *Perfecution*, much lefs what is *intolerable* No *Perfecution :* for it is a Security required in all *Churches* of the World, that thofe who arc intrufted with that Office, fhould obferve the Order and Difcipline that is amongft them. So it was in the *Church of Scotland* whilft *Presbyterian*, where it was refolved, " That whofoever hath born Office " in the Miniftry of the *Kirk*, or that prefently

" bears,

"bears, or shall hereafter bear Office herein, shall
"be charged by every particular *Presbytery* where
"their Residence is, to subscrive the Heads of Di-
"scipline of the *Kirk*, betwixt this and the next
"*Synodal Assemblies* of the *Provinces*, under the
"pain of *Excommunication*; as you may see in *the
Doctrine and Discipline of the Kirk of Scotland*, printed 1641. *pag.* 12. And as they there declared the
Office of a *Bishop* to be unlawful in it self, *pag.* 19.
so I find, that the *General Assembly* did require, that
besides this Subscription to the Book of *Discipline*,
some Persons (I suppose suspected of affection that
way) should subscribe a particular Declaration of
the unlawfulness of *Episcopacy*, as was the Case of
Mr. *Maxwell* and Mr. *Hay*, in *the Principal Acts of
the General Assembly*, 1644. And thus it was amongst
us, when all Persons to be Ordained, were to bring
a Testimonial of their having taken the *Covenant*,
as you may find it in *the Form of Church-Government, pag.* 20. and in all Places required to take it,
and to read the *Directory* the next *Lords-day* after
the receipt of it, by an Ordinance, *Aug.* 23. 1645.
So that taking Security by Profession and Subscription, that the Order of the *Church* shall be obser-
ved by Persons intrusted in the Ministrations of it,
and Suspension in case of refusal, is no *Persecution*.
But supposing that so it was, yet it is not *intolerable.*

ble. I do grant, that it muſt needs be a great trouble to a good Man, that he cannot do *God* and the *Church* that Service which he hath devoted himſelf unto, by reaſon of ſome Limitations put upon him; but yet I think, that this is not ſufficient to carry him oft from Communion with a *Church,* and to ſet up another, becauſe he is denied this Liberty: for he is ſtill capable of being a private Member of it, and therefore he ought to continue in the latter Capacity, when ſuſpended from the former. So ſaith Mr. *Crofton,* in his *Reformation not Separation, Epiſt. to the Reader: I cannot be perſwaded, that I am disbanded from Chriſts Army, ſo ſoon as I am ſuperſeded to my Conduct; I muſt march under his Banner, when I may not be permitted to march at the Head of a Company.* So again, *pag.* 98. *I conceive, Adminiſtration of God's Worſhip is much different from Attendance on God's Worſhip; and I ſtand bound to the laſt, when I am (juſtly or unjuſtly) barred from the firſt.* And this was the Opinion of the *old Nonconformiſts.* But now we find it otherwiſe; and ſometimes *theſe* plead the *obligation of their Ordination,* ſometimes *the Relation which they have to a peculiar People,* and ſometimes *the neceſſity of multitudes of Souls.* The firſt we find inſiſted upon by the Author of *Separation yet no Schiſm, Epiſt. to the Reader : If it be asked, May not Supreme Magi-*
ſtrates,

*ſtrates, within their Dominion, ſuſpend ſome Miniſters
from the Exerciſe of their Office, when they conceive
it is for the peace of the reſt ?* It will be anſwered,
That the Lord of Lords, who giveth the Office and
the Commiſſion ,——— hath certainly with the Office
deſigned them to the Exerciſe thereof, and hath
therein placed, not onely the Office, but the Exerciſe
thereof, above the reſtraint of any Powers whatſo-
ever, ſo long as the Exerciſe thereof continues to be re-
gulated by the Laws of Chriſt. And in this caſe,
nothing is more ordinarily produced than that of
the Apoſtle, *Wo is me, &c.* But is not this to ad-
vance every one beyond the cogniſance of Superiors, and to fall in with the *Church of Rome,* whilſt
they decry it? If indeed theirs was the Apoſtle's
caſe, the Apoſtle's reſolution of *obeying God rather
than Man,* would become them : But how little it
is ſo, let the *old Nonconformiſts* ſhew, in their *Confutation of the Browniſts,* pag. 41. *How unskilfully
that ſpeech of the Apoſtles is alledged, will appear to
them that will conſider theſe three differences between
their Caſe and ours.* 1. *They that inhibited the Apoſtles, were profeſſed Enemies to the Goſpel.* 2. *The
Apoſtles were charged not to teach in the Name of
Chriſt, nor to publiſh any part of the Doctrine of the
Goſpel.* 3. *The Apoſtles received not their Calling and
Authority from men, nor by the hands of men, but*

P

immediately

immediately from God himself ; and therefore might not be restrained or deposed by men : whereas we, though we exercise a Function whereof God is the Author, and we are also called of God to it, yet we are called and ordained by the ministry of men, and may therefore by men be deposed, and restrained from the exercise of it. I shall conclude this with what Mr. *Crofton* faith, in his *Reformation not Separation,* pag. 70. *If the Being of Christianity depended upon my Personal Ministry, as the being or appearing a Christian doth on my Communion with the Church visible, the Inference might be of some force :* But till that be proved, I think it is of little.

But is this really the cafe? Then what becomes of thofe that among themfelves have taken up wholly with other Profeffions, and yet were never charged by their Brethren, for fo doing, (as Mr. *Baxter* is by the Author of the *Antidote, pag.* 15.) *with having left the Lord's Work ?* Now I queftion not, but the fame Reafon that did induce fome to take up with other Employments to the neglect of this, and fo fatisfie the reft, that they acquiefce in it, will alfo be fufficient to fhew, That meer *Ordination* cannot bind to the Exercife of that Office, when the Magiftrate and Church forbids ; and confequently, that a *Reftraint* is no *intolerable Perfecution.*

But *the relation that they have to a peculiar People* makes

makes this Inhibition *intolerable*. This is indeed
pleaded in *Sacrilegious Defertion, pag.* 11. *&* 45.
"I undertake to prove, that Paftors and People are
"the conftitutive Effentials of a true *Church*; that
"Dr. *Seaman*, Mr. *Calamy*, Dr. *Manton*, *&c.* with
"the People fubject to them as Paftors, were true
"*Churches*: Prove you, if you can, that on *Auguft*
"24. 1662. they were degraded, or thefe true
"*Churches* diffolved. But before he puts others to
prove the contrary, he ought to have made good
his own Propofition, by proving, *That the Relation
betwixt particular Paftors and People is not to be diffolved.* For what though Paftors and People are
the Conftitutive Effentials of a true Church? what
though Dr. *Seaman*, Mr. *Calamy*, *&c.* and the People with them, were true Churches? Can neither
Dr. *Seaman*, *&c.* remove, or be removed from a
People, but all this mifchief follows, that Minifters
are prefently degraded, and Churches diffolved?
Could not Mr. *Calamy* remove from St. *Edmonds-
bury* to *Rochford*, and from *Rochford* to *Alderman-
bury*, as he himfelf doth declare in his *Apologie?*
Could not Mr. *Jenkin* remove from *Black-Fryers* to
Chrift-church, without all this diforder? What
wreck was here made in Churches, if this Relation
was indiffoluble? But if a Paftor may thus remove
himfelf from one Church, upon invitation to ano-

P 2   ther,

ther, (as it feems he may) it fhews, that the Relation is not fo ftrict as is pretended ; and that, confequently, Superiors in Church and State may fo
far diffolve that Relation, as well as the Paftor himfelf. But however, what relief will this afford to
thofe that leave thofe Places where they had any
pretence of fuch a Relation, and bufie themfelves
where they had none? What relief will this be to
thofe that contract a new Relation, and that do gather Churches out of Churches? Surely Dr. *Seaman's*, Dr. *Jacomb's*, and Mr. *Jenkin's* Flocks now,
are taken from other Places than *Alhallows Bread-
ftreet, Martins Ludgate, &c.*

Laftly, The *neceffity of the People* is what doth
make their Preaching neceffary (as they would have
it underftood. So *Sacrilegious Defertion, pag. 59.),*
and fo their Sufpenfion *intolerable Perfecution.* But
fuppofing this, (as doubtlefs there is and ever was
Work fufficient for a greater number of skilful and
faithful Labourers) ; yet is there no way to be ufeful, but by facing a numerous Congregation, and
preaching at fuch Times, and in fuch Places, as do
declare a defiance to the Church, which they thereby make a manifeft rupture in, and open feparation from? Is there no good to be done by preaching to Five, befides a Mans own Family, and by
Perfonal Conference and Inftruction? How came
then

then *our Saviour and his Apoftles oftentimes* to betake themfelves to this way, as an Author of their
own, in his *Archippus*, doth inform us, *pag.* 21 ?
But if it be of great advantage, and that *it is no
little part of a Minifters Duty, perfonally to Inftruct,
and Preach from Houfe to Houfe*, as that Author
faith, how comes it to be fo *fadly neglected* by them,
as he there complains? and how comes the Apoftles *Wo* to be pleaded for the one, and not to bind
the other ? Hear what the Author of *Sacrilegious
Defertion* faith, *pag.* 93. "Is it not too much Hy-
"pocrifie to cry out againft them that forbid us
"Preaching, and in the mean time to neglect that
"which none forbids us, *viz. Chriftian Conference.*
Certainly, as he faith, *pag.* 94. *Sincerity inclineth
men to that way of Duty that hath leaft Oftentation.*

But if the ftate of the People be indeed the reafon, why do we not find them where there is moft
need of their Affiftance? Are we not told, in *Sacrilegious Defertion*, pag. 10. *That the Nonconformifts
have found, that fome Places of many Years paft have
had no Minifters at all?* Are there no Places in *England* and *Wales*, that do much more abound in Ignorance, than *London*, and the adjacent Parts ? and
are the *Nonconformifts* there to be met with? No,
that Work is left to one (good Soul) that having
not a Liberty by the Law to exercife his Office in
the

the more Publick way, doth with unwearied dili-
gence purfue the Ends of it, in travelling over fteep
Mountains and craggy Rocks, and converfing with
the rude and untaught Natives, whilft others do
more confult their Eafe and Profit.

You fee then, upon the whole, that their Sufpenfion is not *intolerable Perfecution*, or what will
be fufficient to juftifie their *Separation*; but that
ftill, notwithftanding their Pleas, they are upon
the fame terms with the People; and what will
not juftifie the Separation of the People, will not
juftifie that of the Minifter; and what is fufficient
to retain the People in Communion, is fufficient to
retain the Minifter.

And fo we are left to confider the State of the
People, and whether there be on their part *intole-*
rable Perfecution. Not to difpute whether what is
fuffered be *Perfecution*, or not; I fhall onely confider, whether it be what is fufficient to warrant their
Separation : And that will appear, if we obferve,
That their Suffering muft be either becaufe they do
not at all Communicate with the Church, or that
there are fome particular things onely which they
do not Communicate with us in. If it be for the
former, then they did feparate before their fuffering, and confequently their Suffering can be no reafon for their Separation. If it be onely as to particular

ticular things, then, I fay. it will be hard to fhew,
that any Perfon doth fuffer *intolerably* upon that
fcore; the Church proceeding in fo great tender-
nefs, where Perfons have fhewed their readinefs to
hold Communion with her in what they can, and
have fo far given fatisfaction of their Piety, Peace-
ablenefs, and Compliance, that in the Cafes where
the Laws have been thought fevere, they have rare-
ly been executed upon fuch in their feverity. Which
I conceive is a fufficient Reply to thofe that cry out,
Perfecution, and *intolerable,* becaufe of the great Penalties that Offenders in fuch kind are liable unto.
For, the meer fuppofal and expectation of feverity,
is no good Reafon for Separation, as long as it is
not, nor is likely to be actually inflicted. For, as
Mr. *Bradfhaw* the *Nonconformift,* in his *Unreafona-
blenefs of Separation,* printed 1640. *pag.* 107. doth
fay, *Though Humane Laws, under never fo great Punifhments, fhould bind us to never fo great Corruptions in Gods Service; yet fo long as we do not actually
communicate in thofe Corruptions, our Communicating
is never the worfe for the faid Laws:* So I fay, Though
Laws threaten never fo great Punifhments, yet fo
long as we do not actually fuffer them, our Condition is not the worfe for thefe Laws. And this was
thought a good Argument by Mr. *Baily,* in his *Hi-
ftorical Vindication of the Church of Scotland,* 1646.
pag. 20.

Pag. 20. who, when charged, That the King and his Family are subject to the *Claffical Affemby,* anfwers, *That any* Presbyterian *did ever fo much as begin a Procefs with any Prince, when they had the greateft Provocations thereto, it cannot be fhewed to this day. The Church of* Scotland, *notwithftanding all the crofs Actions of King* James, *or King* Charles,— *yet never did fo much as bethink themfelves of drawing againft them the Sword of Church-Cenfures.* Where he denies not the Charge of their Churches claiming fuch a Power ; but thinks it enough to reply, That fhe had never fo ufed it. So then you fee, that it is not the Power that our Superiors have, nor the Penalties that a Law threatens, that will ferve in this cafe ; as long as the Ufe of that Power, and Execution of thofe Laws is fufpended : and a Perfon ought not any more to quit the Church, than he will his Country, as long as he may be fuffered to abide in it. And that he may do with us, that will hold Communion with our Church in what he can, and doth behave himfelf with modefty in thofe things which for the prefent he cannot Communicate in.

4. *Vnjuft Excommunication* is another Reafon given to make *Separation* warrantable. But that being a *fpiritual Perfecution* (as *Camero* calls it) doth not really differ from the former, and therefore will receive the fame Anfwer.   5. That

5. That which will warrant a *Separation* from a *Church*, is *a neceſſary Communion with it in its Sins.* Towards the reſolution of which, I ſhall obſerve,

1. *That bare Communion with a Church, doth not neceſſarily make a Perſon to communicate with the Sins of it.* This is granted by all that ſay, We muſt not ſeparate from a Church, becauſe of the *ungodly* that are in its Communion, or becauſe of ſome *mixtures* that are in its Worſhip : And if we muſt not ſeparate from them, it is certain we may continue there, without being guilty of the Sin of them. How far the firſt of theſe is and ought to be acknowledged, I have ſhewed above, at *pag.* 62. And how far the latter, you may ſee in Mr. *Brinſley's Arraignment of Schiſm,* pag. 50. *Though toleration of ſome unwarrantable mixtures in a Church, be an evil; yet it is not ſo great an evil, as Separation upon that ground.* This was the Opinion of the Five diſſenting Brethren, in their *Apologetical Narration,* pag. 6. *We have always profeſſed, and that in thoſe times when the Churches of* England *were the moſt either actually over-ſpread with defilements, or in the greateſt danger thereof,— That we both did and would hold a Communion with them, as the Churches of Chriſt.* And this they agreed to, upon this conſideration, that otherwiſe there hath been no Church yet, nor will be to the day of Judgment, which Perſons

Q   otherwiſe

otherwife perfwaded, could or can hold Communion with ; as you may find it in the *old Nonconformifts Letters* to thofe of *New-England*, pag. 12.
Mr. *Firmin's Separation examined*, pag. 25. and *the
Vindication of the Provincial Affembly*, pag. 135.

2. I add, *That the impofition of things unlawful,
or fo thought to be, in a Church, makes a Perfon in
this cafe no farther concerned, than as they are impofed
on him.* For, if Corruptions *tolerated* are no bar to
Communion, then they are not when *impofed*; meer
Impofition not altering the Nature, as Mr. *Crofton* faith,
in his *Jerubbaal*, pag. 27.

3. *Impofition in fome things unlawful, or fuppofed
fo to be, will not juftifie a feparation from what is lawful.* The Author of *Separation yet no Schifm*, in his
Epiftle to the Reader, thus pleads for the People :
" The People are not always free from fuch Impo-
" fitions which they extremely fufpect as finful ; as
" that they cannot enjoy *Baptifm* for their Chil-
" dren without the *Crofs*, nor receive the *Lords*
" *Supper* without *Kneeling* ; to name no more, (as
well he could not). But fuppofe that thefe things
are impofed , and what they extremely fufpect ;
can this be a Reafon for their feparation in thofe
things where nothing of this nature is ? Certainly,
in obedience to Magiftrates, and for Communion
with a Church, we ought to go as far as we can ;
and

and what I cannot do, is no excuse for the omiffion
of what I can. Thus did the *old Nonconformifts*
think and practice, as I obferved to you before,
from the *Vindication of the Provincial Affembly*, pag.
135. *That though fome of them thought it unlawful
to receive the Sacrament kneeling, yet they held Communion with the Church in the reft.* And accordingly Mr. *Firmin* argues, in his *Separation examined*,
pag. 29. *Suppofe there fhould be fome Humane mixtures,
are all the Ordinances polluted ? Why do you not communicate with them in thofe Ordinances which are
pure ?*

Now if this be true, what fhall we fay to them
that have nothing to object againft the greateft part
of what they are required to communicate with us
in ; and yet keep up a total and pofitive Separation from us, as if all Parts were alike infected, and
that from the Crown of the Head, to the Sole of
the Foot, there was nothing but Wounds and pu-
trifying Sores ?

4. *The meer fufpicion that a Perfon may have of
the unlawfulnefs of what is impofed, will not juftifie
his omiffion of, or feparation in that particular.* For,
he ought to come to fome refolution in it, and in
cafe of Obedience, Communion, and Charity, to go
againft fuch his Sufpicion. To this purpofe fpeaks
Mr. *Geree*, in his *Refolution of Ten Cafes*, 1644.

" Things

" Things wherein doubts arife, are of a double na-
"ture : 1. Meerly arbitrary, and at my own di-
" fpofe : 2. That are under command ; as coming
" to the Sacrament, Obedience to the Higher Pow-
"ers in things lawful. If Scruples arife about thefe,
" and a Man doubts he fins if he acts, and he alfo
" doubts he fins if he forbears, &c. In this cafe he
" muft weigh the Scales, and where he apprehends
" moft weight of Reafon, muft incline that way,
" though the other Scale be not altogether empty.
" And this done, after humble and diligent fearch,
" with bewailing our infirmity, that we are no more
" difcerning, will be accepted by God : God puts
" not his People on neceffity of finning, nor can our
" Scruples difpenfe with his Commands. So Mr. *Fal-
do*, in his *Quakerifm no Chriftianity*, pag. 93. " In
" doubtful and difficult Cafes, wherein we cannot
" reach the knowledge of our Duty, it's our Duty
" to follow the Examples of the greateft number
" of the Saints, &c. And then furely, what will
ferve in fuch a cafe to let us difpenfe with our
Doubts, will much more in Obedience to Gover-
nours, and for Communion with a Church. This I
thought to have more largely handled, as it's
thought a new and late Argument, ufed by Bifhop
Sanderfon, &c. (but what I can prove to be of old
the common Refolution of the Cafe), and as the
                                    contrary

contrary is pleaded for from Mr. *Hales*: But lighting happily upon a Book called Mr. *Hales's Treatife of Schifm examined*, wrote by a Learned Perfon, I fhall refer you to it, where he particularly undertakes this Point, *pag.* 110, *&c.*

Having thus made good the Three Propofitions abovefaid, and fhewed, *That the Church of* England *is a True Church*; *That there is a Separation from it*; and, *That this Separation is voluntary and unneceffary*: that which remains is not to be denied, *viz. That therefore the prefent Separation is Schifmatical.* So that now you may fee in what condition thofe of our diffenting Brethren are, that withdraw from the Communion of our Church; and how little able they will be to reconcile their prefent Proceedings, to their former Principles and Profeffions. It was once faid by them, in the *Vindication of the Presbyterial Government*, pag. 133. *We dare not make feparation from a true Church, by departing from it, as you do*, [fpeaking to the *Independents.*] Then *Independency* was what they proved to be *Schifm*, becaufe, 1. *Independents do depart from our Churches, being true Churches, and fo acknowledged by themfelves.* 2. *They draw and feduce Members from our Congregations.* 3. *They erect feparate Congregations.* 4. *They refufe Communion with our Churches in the Sacraments. Now we judge, that no Schifm is to be tolera-*

ted

tcd *in the Church* ; as fay the *London-Minifters*, in their *Letter to the Affembly, pag.* 3. Then the inevitable Confequences of it could be difcovered and reprefented, as that by it *Peoples minds would be troubled, and in danger to be fubverted* ; *bitter heart-burning would be fomented and perpetuated* ; *godly, painful, and orthodox Minifters be difcouraged, and defpifed* ; *the life and power of Godlinefs be eaten out, by frivolous Difputes* ; *and the whole Courfe of Religion in private Families be interrupted, and undermined*; as they there fay, *pag.* 4. Then *Church-Divifion was as great a Sin as Adultery and Theft*, as Dr. *Bryan* maintains, in *the Publick Difputation at Kilingworth*, 1655. *pag.* 28. Then it was pleaded, That they *Covenanted not onely againft Sin, but Schifm*, as faith Mr. *Watfon*, in his *Anatomy upon the Heart, pag.* 160. But is not that now true, which he there charges upon themfelves, *We have gone againft the Letter of it ?* For, do not many of them that have faid all this, *fet up Churches againft Churches, exercife the Worfhip of God, adminifter Ordinances, the Word, Sacraments, apart, and in a feparated Body? Which in a peculiar manner, and by way of eminency, is called Schifm,* faith Mr. *Brinfley*, pag. 16. Is *Schifm* all on a fudden grown fo innocent a thing, that Perfons are to be indulged, and tamely permitted to continue in it ? And is it not as *fad* now, as it was
then,

then, that *many that pretend to Religion, make no Confcience of Schifm*, as Dr. *Manton* on *Jude*, pag. 492. doth obferve ? Certainly, That ftill remains good which was faid by Mr. *Brinfley*, pag. 17. *The Schifms and Divifions which are broken in, and that amongst God's own People, are what I cannot but look upon as one of the blackeft Clouds, one of the faddeft Judgments which hang over the head of this Kingdom at this day ; of fad influence for the prefent, and, un-lefs they be healed, of dangerous confequence for the future.* Have we not *Atheifm*, and *Infidelity*, and *Profanenefs* enough to encounter ; but muft we have more Work found us, by thofe that have given us Arguments to oppofe themfelves with ? Are we in no danger of being over-run with a Foreign Power, and *that the Romans fhall come and take away our Name and Church*; when we, which are at difference amongft our felves, fhall without any oppofition be fwallowed up by them ? Are they yet to be taught, that as nothing can, fo nothing will fooner make us a prey to them, than mutual Hoftilities amongft our felves ? And whence is it, that they will run the adventure, and care not what they expofe us to ? Is it that *Rome* is nearer to them, than they are to us ? That will not be fuppofed. Is it that they ex-pect better Quarter from that, than they meet with from our Church ? That let Experience decide. Is

it

it that by bringing all to confufion, and a common fcramble, they may hope to go away with the Supremacy? That their Divifions amongft themfelves doth confute. For, can they think, becaufe they agree againft us, that they will agree among themfelves? Or, can they think, if they do not, that one alone can carry the Victory from the Common Enemy? Let a fober Author of their own, in his *Difcourfe of the Religion of England*, be heard, who faith, *pag.* 39. *That the common fafety and advancement of true Religion cannot ftand by a multiplicity of petty Forms ; but requires an ample and well-fetled State, to defend and propagate it againft the amplitude and potency of the Romifh Intereft.* And are not thefe the thoughts of the wifeft in this Nation? and fhall Men yet continue to keep up Feuds and Animofities, and make no fcruple of contradicting themfelves to feed them?' It was once faid by Mr. *Brinfley, pag.* 62. That *it's a foul blemifh to a Minifter of Chrift, to fpeak one thing to day, and another thing to morrow, to fay and unfay.* And I will appeal to all the World, whether this be not what our Brethren are guilty of. Surely, if they would but take the pains to review what they have written, and weigh thofe Arguments againft *Schifm* and *Separation* that they formerly publifhed, they would return to themfelves, and to that *Church* which they have fo unadvifedly

advisedly broken off from ; they would then think
it their Duty, with the *old Nonconformists*, to come
as far as they can, and their Happiness to live in
the Communion of that *Church* where they may be
as good as they will ; they would then see, that
Schifm is a great Sin, and that their *present Separa-*
tion is *Schifm*.

I should now conclude, but that I may fear that
Mr. *Jenkin* will proclaim ; and others think me a
Slanderer, for saying, *pag.* 44. That he hath borrowed the Substance of this *Sermon* from Mr. *Brinsley's*
Arraignment of Schifm, if I do not make it good :
and therefore in my own vindication, and also to
shew you how far *holiness and indignation* may be
pretended, when indeed it is little better than *hypo-*
crisie and calumny that prompts Men on, I shall draw
the Comparison, and leave you and all others to
judge, whether he be not one of those *empty and*
unaccomplished Predicants spoken of in his *Exodus*,
pag. 56. *that preach the Sermons of others*, and, more
than that, dare before all the World publish them
as his own : the like to which is also done by him,
or one of his Brethren, in the *Vindication of the*
Presbyterial Government, *pag.* 132. compared with
Mr. *Brinsley*, *pag.* 16. and *pag.* 134. with 52. and
pag. 135. with 41. Nor hath he borrowed from
Mr. *Brinsley* alone, but hath rifled divers other Au-

R   thors

thors for the greateſt part of his Book, as might ea-
ſily be proved, were it either requiſite, or worth
the while. How far he is beholden to others for
that kind of Wit and tawdry Eloquence that a groſs
and bribed Flatterer, in his *Patronus bonæ Fidei,*
gives him the Title of *Seneca* for, the Author of
the Vindication of the Conforming Clergie hath already ſhewed : And how bold he hath made with
others for Argument and Reaſon, the following In-
ſtances will be a ſufficient *Specimen*, where he hath
ſcarcely left any thing untouched that he then
thought might ſerve his purpoſe.

A Sermon

A Sermon preached by W. Jenkin, *herewith Printed, and also to be found in his* Comment on Jude, *printed in* Quarto, 1652.	The Arraignment of the prefent Schifm, by *John Brinſley.* LONDON, 1646.

THeir Herefies were perverfe and damnable Opinions; their Schifm was a perverfe Separation from Churchcommunion : The former was in Doctrinals, the latter in Practicals; the former was oppofite to Faith, this latter to Charity. By Faith all the Members are united to the Head, by Charity one to another : and as the breaking of the former is Herefie, fo their breaking of the latter was Schifm. *pag.* 21.

Schifm is ufually faid to be twofold, negative, and pofitive. 1. Negative is, when there is onely *fimplex feceſſio,* when there is onely a bare feceſſion, a peaceable and quiet withdrawing from Communion with a Church, without making any head againft that Church from which the departure is. 2. Pofitive is, when perfons fo withdrawing do fo confociate and draw themfelves into a diftinct and oppofite Body, fetting up a Church againft a Church, or, as Divines exprefs it, from

HErefic (*faith* Jerome) is properly a perverfe Opinion, Schifm is a perverfe Separation. *The one a Doctrinal, the other a practical Error. The one oppofite to Faith, the other to Charity.. -By the one (Faith) all the Members are united to the Head; by the other (Charity) they are united to one another. Now the breaking of the firft of thefe Bands is Herefie, the latter Schifm.* pag. 14.

*There is, to ufe his terms (*Camero), *a negative and a pofitive Separation. The former is fimplex feceſſio, when one or more do quietly and peaceably withdraw themfelves from Communion with a Church,—— not making head againft that Church from which they are departed : The other, when perfons fo withdrawing do confociate and draw themfelves into a diftinct and oppofite Body, fetting up a Church againft a Church. —— This is that which* Auguftine, *and other Divines after him, call the fet-*

ting

Mr. Jenkin.

from *Augustine,* an Altar againſt an Altar. And this is it which in a peculiar manner, and by way of eminency, is called by the name of Schiſm. pag. 22.

Schiſm becomes ſinful, either in reſpect, 1. of the groundleſneſs; or, 2. the manner thereof. 1. The groundleſneſs; when there is no caſting of perſons out of the Church by an unjuſt Cenſure of Excommunication, no departure by unſufferable Perſecution, no Hereſie nor Idolatry in the Church maintained. 2. The manner of Separation makes it unlawful; when 'tis made without due endeavour, and waiting for Reformation of the Church from which the departure is: and ſuch a raſh departure is againſt Charity, which ſuffers both much and long all tolerable things: It is not preſently diſtaſted, when the juſteſt occaſion is given; it firſt uſeth all poſſible means of remedy. The Chyrurgeon reſerves Diſmembring as the laſt remedy. It looks upon a ſudden breaking off from Communion with a Church (which is a diſmembring) not as Chyrurgery, but Butchery. pag. 23.

I ſhall not ſpend time to compare it with Hereſie, though ſome have

Mr. Brinſley.

ting up of an *Altar againſt an Altar.* And this is it (ſaith that judicious Author) which in a peculiar manner, and by way of eminency, is called by the name of Schiſm. pag. 16.

Unwarrantable, either for ground, or manner; The former an unjuſt, the latter a raſh Separation; each a Schiſm. Unjuſt, when there is no Perſecution, no ſpreading Error or Hereſie, no Idolatry. 2. The manner, which if ſudden and heady, without due endeavour and expectance of Reformation in that Church, it may be a raſh, and conſequently an unwarrantable Separation, inaſmuch as it is oppoſite to Charity, —it being the nature of Charity to ſuffer much and long,—all things which are ſufferable:—It is not preſently diſtaſted, ſo as to fly off upon every ſmall and trivial occaſion; no nor yet upon a juſt and weighty one, without firſt aſſaying all poſſible means of remedy. So deals the wary and careful Chyrurgeon with his Patient; not preſently fall to diſmembring,—reſerving it for the laſt remedy. So deals Charity by the Church; not preſently ſeparate and break off Communion (which is the diſmembring of a Church.) No, this (ſaith Camero) is not Chyrurgia, but Carnificina; which Mr. Cotton ··· engliſheth rightly, not Chyrurgery, but Butchery. pag. 24, 25.

Muſculus informs me of ſome who in point of ſinfulneſs have compared Schiſm

Mr Jenkin.

have faid that Schifm is the greater fin of the two. *Aug. contr. Don.l.2. c.6.* tells the *Donatifts*, that Schifm was a greater fin than that of the *Traditores*, who in time of Perfecution, through fear, delivered their Bibles to Perfecutors to be burnt. A fin at which the *Donatifts* took fo much offence, that it was the ground of their Separation. *pag.*24.

In refpect of Chrift, 1. It's an horrible indignity offered to his Body (as the Apoftle fpeaks, 1 *Cor.* 1. 15.) and makes him to appear the Head of two Bodies. How monftrous and difhonourable is the very conceit hereof! 2. It's rebellion againft his Command, his great Command of Love. The Grace of Love is by fome called the Queen of Graces; and it's greater than Faith in refpect of its Object, not God onely, but Man; its Duration, which is eternal; its manner of working, not in a way of receiving Chrift (as Faith), but of giving the Soul to him. *pag.* 24.

By Divifions among our felves, we endeavour to divide our felves from him, in and from whom is all our fulnefs.——Upon the Stock of Schifm commonly Herefie is grafted. There is no Schifm (faith *Jerome*)

Mr Brinfley.

Schifm with Herefie, and others who have aggravated it beyond it, as the greater evil of the two. Auguftine *tells the* Donatifts, contr. Don. l. 2. c. 6. *that their Schifm was a greater fin than that which they took fuch high offence at, and which was the ground of their feperation* (viz. *the fin of the* Traditores, *fuch as in time of Perfecution had through fear delivered up their Bibles to the Perfecutors to be burnt.*) pag. 17, 18.

It is injurious to Chrift, *who feemeth by this means to be as it were divided. So* Paul *urgeth it,* Is Chrift divided? —— Himfelf *hereby made the Head of two difagreeing Bodies; which is difhonourable, and monftrous to conceive of him.* pag. 19.

It's oppofite to fo great a Grace as Charity. Charity, the Queen *of Graces,——greater than Faith,——* 1. In regard of the Object :——Faith refpecteth God onely, but Charity both God and Man. 2. In regard of the manner of working : Faith worketh intramittendo, by receiving and letting in Chrift and his Benefits; but Charity extramittendo, by giving out the Soul.—— 3. In regard of duration :- Charity is for eternity. p. 18.

By dividing themfelves from the Body, they are in a dangerous way to divide themfelves from the Head.---Schifm maketh way to Herefie. So Jerome. *There is no Schifm, but ordinarily it inventeth and broacheth fome*

Mr. *Jenkin.*

rome) but ordinarily it inventeth and produceth fome Herefie, that fo the Separation may feem the more juftifiable. The *Novatians* and *Donatifts* from Schifm fell to Herefies. Our Times fadly comment upon this Truth, they equally arifing unto both. *pag.* 25, 26.

Its. injurious to the peace and quietnefs of the Church.——If the natural Body be divided and torn, pain and fmart muft needs follow. The tearing and rending of the myftical Body, goes to the Heart of all fenfible Members: they often caufe the Feverifh Diftempers of Hatred, Wrath, Seditions, Envying, Murders. Schifm in the Church puts the Members out of joynt; and disjoynted Bones are painful: *All my bones* (faith *David*) *are out of joynt.* Church-Divifions caufe fad thoughts of Heart. *pag.* 27.

It's oppofite to the Edification of the Church. Divifion of Tongues hindred the building of *Babel*; and doubtlefs Divifion in Hearts, Tongues, Hands, and Heads, muft needs hinder the building of *Jerufalem.* While Parties are contending, Churches and Commonwealths fuffer. In troublous times the

Mr. Brinfley.

fome Herefie, that fo the Separation may feem the more juftifiable.—— *A Truth fufficiently experimented in thofe ancient Schifmaticks, the* Novatians *and* Donatifts, *who from Schifm fell to be Authors or Defenders of Heretical Opinions. We have a late and dreadful Inftance, &c.* pag. 22.

The Church is hereby difquieted. Even as it is in the natural Body, if there be a folutio continui, *fo as it be divided, it breedeth fmart and pain.*——*The myftical Body cannot be rent and torn by Divifions, but it goeth to the heart of all the fenfible Members. The divifions of* Reuben *were great thoughts of heart,*——*oftimes breeding thofe Feverifh diftempers of Hatred, Variance, Wrath, Seditions, I and Murders too.* p. 21.

Schifm in the Church puts the Members out of joynt;—— *Bones out of joynt are painful. Thence* David *borrows this expreffion,* All my bones are out of joynt. *Such are Schifms in the Church, caufing fad thoughts of heart.* pag. 67.

The Church is hereby hindred in the Edification of it. We know what it was that hindred the building of Babel, *even a Schifm in their Tongues, divifion of Languages.*——*And furely there is no one thing that can more hinder the building of* Jerufalem,—— *when Chriftians fhall be divided in their Heads, Hearts, Tongues, Hands.* As

Mr. Jenkin.

the Walls and Temple of *Jerusalem* went but flowly on. pag. 27.

When Church-Members are put out of joynt, they are made unferviceable, and unfit to perform their feveral Offices. They who were wont to joyn in Prayer, Sacraments, and Fafting, and were ready to all mutual Offices of Love, are now fallen off from all. pag. 28.

Our Separation(from *Rome*)was not before all means were ufed for the cure and reformation of the *Romanifts*, by the difcovery of their Errours, that poffibly could be thought of: notwithftanding all which (though fome have been enforced to an acknowledgement of them) they ftill obftinately perfift in them. Our famous, godly, and learned Reformers would have healed *Babylon*, but fhe is not healed. Many skilful Phyficians have had her in hand, but fhe grew fo much the worfe.——In ftead of being reclaimed, they anathematized them with the dreadfulleft Curfes, excommunicated, · yea murdered and deftroyed multitudes of thofe who endeavoured their reducement; not permitting any to trade, buy or fell, to have either Religious

Mr. Brinfley.

——*As it is in Civil Wars, whilft the Parties are contending, the Commonwealth fuffers.——The Wall and Temple of* Jerufalem *went flowly on in troublous Times.* pag. 21.

Members of the Church being put out of joynt by Schifm, become unufeful to the Body, unapt to thofe Duties and Services which before they performed. —— How is it that thofe who were wont to joyn with the Churches in Hearing, Prayer, Sacraments, and were fo ready to all mutual Offices of Love, are now fallen off from all? pag. 67.

Our Separation was neceffitated, through their obftinacy in their Errors ; which notwithftanding the difcovery of them, and that fo clear, as that fome of their own have been enforced to an acknowledgement of them, and all ways and means ufed for their Reformation, they ftill perfift in. What then remains, but a cutting off? We would have healed Babylon, but fhe is not healed. What then followeth? Forfake her, and let us go every one to his own Country. How many Phyficians have had her in hand, Luther, &c. and the reft of our pious Reformers ? but all to no purpofe. ——We were enforced—— fhe not permitting any to trade, buy or fell, to have either Religious or Civil Communion with her, except they receive her Mark in their Hands and Foreheads : But, on the other hand,

(128)

Mr. *Jenkin.*

ous or Civil Communion with them, except they received the Beasts Mark in their Hands and Foreheads. All which confidered, we might fafely forfake her.--- Since in stead of healing *Babylon*, we could not be preferved from her deftroying of us, we did defervedly depart from her, and every one go into his own Country: and unlefs we had done fo, we could not have obeyed the clear Precept, *Apoc.* 18. *Come out of her my people.*   pag 29, 30.

To feparate from Congregations where the Word of Truth and Gofpel of Salvation are held out in an ordinary way, as the Proclamations of Princes are held forth upon Pillars, to which they are affixed; where the Light of Truth is fet up, as it were upon a Candleftick, to guide Paffengers to Heaven: to feparate from them, to whom belong the Covenants, and where the Sacraments, the Seals of the Covenant, are for fubftance rightly difpenfed; where Chrift walketh in the midft of his golden Candlefticks, and difcovereth his prefence in his Ordinances, whereby they are made effectual to the converfion and edification of Souls in an ordinary way; where the Members are Saints, by a profeffed fubjection to Chrift,-- where there are fundry who in the judgement of

Mr. Brinfley.

hand, anathematizing them.---Thefe things confidered, let God and the World be judge, whether our Separation from them be voluntary.--- Not unjuft, being warranted by Authority of Scripture, commanding this feparation, Come out of her my People, Rev. 18. 4.   pag. 27, 28.

Are not our Congregations true Churches? What, are not here the Pillars of Truth? Is not the Word of Truth, the Gofpel of Salvation here held forth, and that in an ordinary and conftant way, even as the Edicts and Proclamations of Princes are wont to be held forth by Pillars to which they are affixed? ---where the Light of Gods Truth is fet up and held forth, for the guiding of paffengers in the way to Eternal Life? Are not here the golden Candlefticks, where the Seals of Gods Covenant, the Sacraments of the New Teftament, are for fubftance rightly difpenfed; --- where there is the prefence of Chrift in the midft of his Ordinances, fo as in an ordinary way they are made effectual to the converfion and falvation of many; where Chrift fitteth, walketh in the midft of his golden Candlefticks;

Mr. *Jenkin.*

of Charity may be conceived to have the work of Grace really wrought in their hearts, by walking in some measure answerable to their Profession: I say, to separate from these, as those with whom Church Communion is not to be held, is Schismatical. *pag.* 31, 32.

The voluntary and unnecessary Separation from a true Church, is Schismatical. *pag.* 31.

Pretences for Separation are alledged; frequently, and most plausibly, Mixt Communion, and of admitting into Church-fellowship the vile with the precious, and those who are Chaff, and therefore ought not to lodge with the Wheat.

Answ. 1. Not to insist upon what some have urged, *viz.* That this hath been the Stone at which most Schismaticks have stumbled, and the pretence which they have of old alledged,——as is evident in the examples of the *Audæans, Novatians, Donatists, Anabaptists, Brownists.* *pag.* 33.

2. Let them consider, whether the want of reforming abuses, proceed not from some unhappy obstructions in the exercise of Discipline, rather than from the allowance of the Church.

3. Let them consider, whether when

Mr. Brinsley.

sticks,——where there are Societies of visible Saints, all such by outward profession, and a considerable part of them walking in measure answerable to that profession; can it be questioned, where these are, whether there be true Churches of Christ? *pag.* 29, 30.

Schism is a voluntary and unwarrantable Separation from a true Church. *pag.* 23.

Sinful mixtures are tolerated among you:—— *There is not that due separation of the Wheat from the Chaff, the precious from the vile; but all sorts are admitted.*

Answ. 1. *I might here mind them, That this hath been the common Stock whereupon Schism hath been usually grafted, the common pretence taken up by all Schismaticks,*——the Novatians, Audæans, Donatists:——*from the same Root sprung that later Schism of the* Anabaptists:——*It was the same Stone at which* Brown *and his Followers first stumbled.* pag. 37, 38, 39.

What though there are some failings in the execution, through some unhappy obstructions in the exercise of Discipline? yet cannot the Church stand charged with them. pag. 40.

Consider the manner in separating

S   *at*

Mr. Jenkin.

when they feparate from Sinful mixtures, the Church be not at that very time purging out thofe Sinful mixtures. pag. 33.

Hath not God his Church, even where corruption of Manners hath crept into a Church, if purity of Doctrine be maintained? And is feparation from that Church lawful, from which God doth not feparate? pag. 34.

Let them confider, whether God hath made private Chriftians Stewards in his Houfe, to determine whether thofe with whom they communicate are fit Members of the Church, or not? or rather, whether it be not their duty, when they difcover Tares in the Church, in ftead of feparating from it, to labour that they may be found good Corn ; that fo when God fhall come to gather his Corn in to his Garner, they may not be thrown out? Church-Officers are Minifterially betrufted with the ordering of the Church, and for the opening and fhutting of the Doors of the Churches Communion, by the Keys of Doctrine and Difcipline; and herein if they fhall be either hindred, or negligent, private Chriftians fhall not be intangled in the guilt of their Sin. p. 34, 35.

Mr. Brinfley.

at fuch a time, in a time of Reformation.——What, feparate from a reforming Church? pag. 51, 52.

Suppofe there may be fome, nay many juft Scandals amongft us, by reafon of corruption of manners; yet is not this a fufficient ground of feparation from a Church wherein there is purity of Doctrine. pag. 50. How dare any forfake that Church which God hath not forfaken? p. 59. God hath not made all private Chriftians Stewards, nor yet Surveyors in his Houfe, fo as that every one fhould take an exact notice of the conditions of all thofe whom they hold Communion with, who are fit to be members of the Church, and who not. It is Cyprian's counfel. What though there be fome Tares difcovered in the Church,——yet let us, for our parts, labour that we may be found good Corn, that fo when God fhall come to gather his Crop into his Garner, we may not be caft out. —— Minifterially the Church-Officers, whom Chrift hath betrufted with the ordering of the Church, them he hath made the Porters in his Houfe, for the opening and fhutting the doors of the Churches Communion, by the keys of Doctrine and Difcipline. Now, in this cafe, if either their hands be tied by any humane reftrictions,——or if through negligence they let loofe the Rains, how

private Chriftians fhould be entangled in the guilt of that fin, it cannot be conceived. pag. 414. The

Mr. Jenkin.

The Command *not to eat with a Brother, &c. 1 Cor. 5. 11.* concerns not Religious but Civil Communion, by a voluntary, familiar, intimate Conversation, either in being invited, or inviting. *pag.* 35.

Now though such Civil eating was to be forborn, yet it follows not at all, much less much more, that Religious eating is forbidden : Because, Civil eating is arbitrary and unnecessary ; not so Religious, which is enjoyned, and a commanded Duty. *pag.* 36.

It should be our care to prevent Separation : To this end,

1. Labour to be progressive in the work of Mortification. *pag.* 38.

2. Admire no Mans Person.—— This caused the *Corinthian* Schism. Take heed of Man-worship.

3. Labour for Experimental benefit by the Ordinances.—— Find the setting up of Christ in your hearts by the Ministry, and then you will not dare to account it Antichristian. If with *Jacob*, we could say of our *Bethels, God is here,* we would set up Pillars.

4. Neither give nor receive Scandals. Give them not, to occasion

Mr. Brinsley.

That which Paul *prohibits there, is not properly a Religious, but a Civil Communion, not to mingle themselves with such scandalous Livers, by a voluntary, familiar, and intimate Conversation,——in an ordinary way, repairing to their Tables, or inviting them to yours.*

If we may not have Civil, much less Religious Communion. Ans. Not so neither ; inasmuch as the one is arbitrary and voluntary, the other a necessary Communion. pag. 45.

How shall this Unity be attained ?
1. *To this end labour after new hearts.*

How may Schism be prevented ?
6. *Take heed of having the Persons of Men in admiration. This occasioned all those Divisions in the Church of* Corinth.——*Take we heed how we look too much at Men.* p. 59.

4. *Labour to see and acknowledge God in our Congregations.——Now if he be here, how dare any withdraw ? When* Jacob *apprehended God present with him at* Bethel, (Surely the Lord is in this place.) *he sets up his Pillar there.——Have we met with him ? why do we not set up our Pillar here ?* pag. 58.

3. *Take heed of Scandals, whether of giving or receiving: Of giving,*

to

Mr. Jenkin.	Mr. Brinfley.

Mr. Jenkin.

fion others to feparate ; nor receive them, to occafion thy own Sepa-ration.—— Conftrue doubtful mat-ters charitably. Look not upon Blemifhes with Multiplying-glaff.s, or old Mens Spectacles : Hide them, though not imitate them. Sport not your felves with others nakednefs.

5. Be not much taken with Novelties. New-Lights have fet this Church on fire. For the moft part they are taken out of the Dark-Lanthorns of old Hereticks. They are falfe and Fools-fires, to lead Men into the Precipice of Se-paration. Love Truth in an old drefs ; let not Antiquity be a pre-judice againft, nor Novelty an in-ducement to the entertainment of Truth.

6., Give not way to leffer diffe-rences : A little divifion will foon rife up to a greater. Small Wedg-es make way for bigger. Our hearts are like to Tinder, a little fpark will enflame them. Be je-lous of your hearts.—— *Paul* and *Barnabas* feparated about a fmall matter, the taking of an Affociate. *pag.* 40, *&c.*

Mr. Brinfley.

to drive off others ; of receiving, to fet off our felves.—— Doubtful mat-ters ftill conftrue them on the better part ; So doth Charity ; not looking upon Blemifhes with Multiplying or Magnifying-glaffes. ——So far as may be without fin, hide them. —— Curfed Cham efp'es the nakednefs of his Father, and makes fport with it.

pag. 56.

2. Be not over-affected with No-velties ——At for thofe New Lights which have fet this Kingdom on fire at this day, for the moft part they are no other than what have been ta-ken out of the Dark-Lanthorns of former Hereticks,——no other but ig-nes fatui, falfe fires, ufeful onely to miflead.——Truth is lovely, and ought to be embraced in whatever drefs fhe cometh, whether new or old. As not Antiquity, fo neither fhould Novelty be any prejudice to Verity.

1. Take heed of leffer divifions. Small Wedges make way for great ones. Small differences fometimes rife to Divifions. pag. 57.

4. Be jealous over our own hearts ; they being like unto Tinder, ready to take fire by the leaft fpark.——It was no great matter that Paul and Bar-nabas differed upon, onely about the taking of an Affociate. pag. 71, &c.

Now,

Now, *Sir*, by this you may perceive, how fome Men do make their Books and Sermons, and by what ways a Man may rife to the reputation of being a confiderable Author : he may cull and pick, pilfer and fteal, and become Learned to a miracle, an excellent Preacher, and write even to a *Folio* ; and if he had but the Art of keeping men from poring into neglected Authors, and prying into Books that are caft into corners, might pafs as fuch : But as long as what is forgotten in one Age, is revived in another, and as long as it is become a Trade to collect *Pamphlets*, I would advife your Friend to be more wary for the future, and keep from writing a *Folio* and a *Comment* again.

And now, *Sir*, it is high time for me to con-clude, to whom it is no pleafure to deal in fuch a way, and to converfe with thofe kind of Books that you fee my Defign hath put me upon. It is Charity to you and the World that hath led me along ; and I hope I have fo managed it, as fhall be to the offence of none, but thofe that are Enemes to Truth : I am fure I have fo much avoided all that might exafperate, that I have for that reafon caft afide Leaves of what fome others might be tempted to have taken in. If Mr. *Jenkin* hath been hardly dealt with, he muft thank himfelf, who having, without provocation, defamed others, could not be fuffered to run away with that out-cry which he hath made, without a juft Rebuke. I am,

(*S I R*)

Your Servant,

S. R.

F I N I S.

www.ingramcontent.com/pod-product-compliance
Lightning Source LLC
Chambersburg PA
CBHW032007010726
47493CB00007B/2310